WAGON TRAILS
AND
WAGGIN' TAILS

The story of four dogs and the wagon train that took them on the 2000 mile journey from Independence, Missouri to the Willamette Valley in Oregon in the year 1850.

By R. L. Peters

ISBN 978-1-7335515-2-6

Table of Contents

FOREWARD

The Oregon Trail was the route originally followed by trappers and fur traders in the early 1800s to reach their trapping grounds in the northwest and then to return east in the fall with their furs. It was not heavily traveled until about 1843 when the migration west attracted larger and larger numbers of pioneers. It passed through what would later become the states of Kansas, Nebraska, Wyoming, and Idaho before reaching the Willamette Valley in what is now the state of Oregon. Only Missouri, the official starting point of the trail was a state in 1850, the year our story takes place. The land in between was known then only as Unorganized Territory.

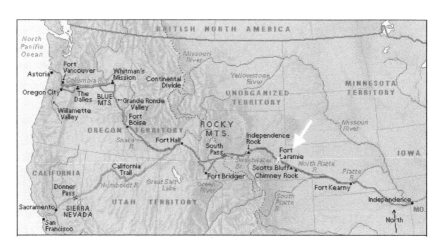

The Oregon Trail

During the mid-1800s approximately 400,000 pioneers traveled along parts of the Oregon Trail, most of them starting in Independence, Missouri. Some headed southwest to New Mexico on the Sante Fe Trail after only a few days on the trail. The majority turned southwest to Utah and California on the Mormon and California Trails much further along the way. This is the story of a wagon train that did just that and the four dogs that traveled west with it. It is part history lesson and part travelogue with a sprinkling of wildlife facts, but it is mostly about the adventures and hardships the dogs shared with their fellow travelers. I hope the reader finds this mix of subjects both informative and entertaining. For those who make it to the end of the trail, don't stop there. The appendices contain summaries of several of the subjects introduced along the way.

CHAPTER 1 - WAGONS HO!

The mood of the large group of people gathered in a field on the edge of town was one of optimism, excitement, and anxiety. It was the day before a caravan of seventy covered wagons would leave Independence, Missouri and begin the long journey west along the Oregon Trail to Oregon City. Everyone was busily packing food and other supplies, inspecting their wagons one last time, and tending to the mules and oxen that would pull them westward. Several men were checking on a nearby herd of cattle that would accompany the train. It was the spring of 1850. The wagons would have to travel almost 2000 miles through prairies and deserts, over mountains, and across many rivers to reach their destination. If all went as planned, the trip would last four or five months and end before the cold weather arrived in the mountains of the far west. Many had made this journey before them, but it would be a new and unfamiliar experience for those about to leave Independence for the first time and a growing tension among the wagon owners could be felt by all as the day of departure approached.

Independence was the most popular starting point for the journey west because everything an emigrant would need to make the trip could be purchased there - wagons, animals, food, tools, and other necessities. It was also a Missouri River port to which the pioneers and their wagons, possessions, and animals could be transported by steamboat from St. Louis and other points east. The two hundred mile upstream trip from St. Louis to Independence was an easy one that took little time. During the early spring thousands of people arrived in Independence to join a wagon train heading west. The camping areas around the city were crowded with wagons organizing into separate trains. It was important for the trains to leave at about the same time and so their leaders had to decide among themselves exactly when each would depart. If one left too early, the grasses on which the oxen and cattle relied on for food would not yet be available. If one left too late, an early winter in the mountains of Oregon would be disastrous.

Earlier that week an election was held to select the leader of the train and others that would serve as officers. The election was just a formality as almost everyone knew that the man they called Captain Billy would lead them along the trail. Billy was the most experienced person in the group and had successfully led a train of similar size west two years earlier. He was there specifically to serve as the train's captain. Billy was an older man who had never settled down to a permanent home. He had no family and traveled alone. Billy considered the job of trail boss as a good a way as any other of making a living and a train of this size meant a good payday.

On that last night in Independence Billy held a meeting with all of the wagon owners to review the train's written rules and regulations, the manner in which disagreements would be resolved, the restrictions on gambling and drinking, and the penalties for rule violations. He also conducted a type of lottery to determine the order in which the wagons would travel. It was best to be near the front of the train and the lucky ones got those positions.

Captain Billy took this opportunity as well to warn everyone to pack only those supplies which would be needed to survive the trip. He passed out a written list of recommended items that included food items, cooking utensils, tools and equipment, medical supplies, clothing, bedding, tents, and weapons. He advised the men not to pack more than a few luxury and personal items at the expense of necessities, but knew from experience that more than likely many would ignore his advice. Spare wagon axles and other items to be shared by all or sold to anyone with the cash to buy them would be carried in two large supply wagons. These wagons also carried a number of things that could be traded for food or clothing with the Indians the train would surely encounter along the way.

Billy also used this final meeting to warn the men of the dangers their families could encounter on the trail. He reminded them that one of every ten people who start the journey do not finish it. He told them that most of the people who die on the trail do so because they contract a fatal disease, primarily cholera. Other diseases like smallpox and diphtheria took the lives of many children. Clean drinking water was often scarce and it was not uncommon for travelers to drink from rivers or streams that had been contaminated by the wagon trains and cattle traveling ahead of them. Cholera outbreaks were devastating and affected all that drank from an infected water source. Contracting the disease on the trail usually ended in a quick death. He went on to say that others die of accidental shootings and that more than a few young children fall from their wagon, are run over, and die of their injuries. Billy told them that supply shortages are always unexpected, but that the loss of even one supply wagon or poor hunting conditions along the way could lead to a scarcity of food. He explained that bad weather, river crossing mishaps, a lack of fuel for fires, thefts by bandits, wagon accidents, and skirmishes with Indians were not only possible, but likely, although these problems were much less likely to be a threat to their lives than disease and starvation. Billy ended his speech with this simple advice - "Be careful, stay clean, and conserve supplies".

A young girl named Missy Marshall watched the activity in the camp from her perch on the driver's seat of her family's wagon. Missy was only ten years old, but her long blonde hair and pretty face made her look much older. She was doing her best just to stay out of the way while her mother and father worked to prepare for the trip. Next to her sat her dog Halo, a tan and black terrier that Missy got as a puppy three years earlier. She named her Halo because before she had a name Missy called Halo her little angel. Halo was a small dog with a thick wiry coat, bushy eyebrows, and a shaggy beard. In spite of her scruffy appearance Halo was

4

friendly and affectionate and she and Missy were inseparable friends. Halo's ancestors were bred to hunt foxes on the England-Scotland border and later came to be known as Border Terriers. Halo, however, was not much of a hunter. Missy's mother and father, John and Emma, also thought the world of Halo and, although they were concerned that the trip might be difficult for her, never considered leaving her behind.

Halo

The Marshalls had made a similar journey fifteen years earlier when John and Emma moved from the east coast to Ohio to become farmers. They grew corn, wheat, and potatoes on 150 acres of rich farmland and raised pigs for sale to local markets. The pigs ate the corn and the Marshalls ate the potatoes and the pigs. John was smarter and more industrious than most of his peers and his farm was very successful as small farms go. He believed, however, that competition from the ever increasing numbers of farmers moving into Ohio would eventually depress the prices of his two cash crops, wheat and pork. He considered farming in the upper Midwest, but reports of the difficulties experienced by those that had were discouraging. Droughts and insect swarms were common, the winters were often severe, the summers were hot and humid, sources of wood were scarce, and the prairie sod was hard to plow and to plant. He decided in the end that his family would be happier and their future more secure in the far west.

Once the order in which the wagons would travel was established John made time to introduce himself to the wagon owners that would be traveling immediately ahead of and behind his wagon in the caravan. Ryan and Neva Walsh were the owners of one of these wagons. Ryan and Neva were brother and sister. They had emigrated from Ireland four years earlier when they were in their mid-twenties. The failure of the potato crop in Ireland at that time resulted in widespread starvation and disease that took the lives of nearly a million people and forced another million people to leave the country. The Great Irish Potato Famine lasted for nearly five years.

Ryan and Neva were two of the nearly 650,000 Irish immigrants that arrived in New York City alone during the famine years. Most of the new arrivals were unskilled, could not read or write, and held menial, low wage jobs. Ryan and Neva were exceptions. Both were literate and possessed trade skills, yet life in New York was a constant struggle for the two new arrivals and they soon decided to escape the squalid living conditions, crime, disease, and growing intolerance that the immigrants faced daily in New York by joining the migration west. It took three years of hard work to scrape together the money needed to begin the journey and Ryan worried that it was still not enough to see them through to its end. He hoped that they would find enough food along the way to make up for any shortfall in their supplies.

The day before they were to leave New York Neva noticed a dog scrounging through garbage cans outside of their rented room looking for something to eat. Although she had little to offer the dog but pity, she reluctantly took the little fellow in thinking that he deserved to escape the city as much as they did. He was a Scottish terrier and so Neva gave him a very Scottish name, Angus. She guessed he was maybe four or five years old. He had the thick, black, curly coat and very short legs characteristic of his breed. He seemed to be well-bred and in much better shape than one would expect for a stray and Neva figured he had somehow become separated from his owners. He seemed happy just to have found a new home and began the trek west with Ryan and Neva as though he belonged with them. By the time the three of them had reached Independence, Angus was answering to his new name.

Wandering among the wagons was yet another dog that seemed to be searching for food. She was a young Australian shepherd with a long, beautiful coat of white, tan, and brown patches. She had lived on a farm in

7

Independence for the first few years of her life, but was left behind to take care of herself when her owners decided to travel west with an earlier wagon train. Even though her breed originated only a few years

Angus

earlier in the United States and not Australia, she had been given the name Aussie by the farmer, but of course no one knew that now. Aside from the occasional handout she fed herself by hunting small animals, a skill at which she had become quite good. She spent much of her time around the cattle and the men responsible for the herd came to know her well in the days leading up to the train's departure. They called her Dewdrop because she slept each night in the long grass that was wet with early morning dew at that time of year. Soon after the cattlemen arrived each morning

Dewdrop began her work keeping the herd together. In return the men brought her bacon for breakfast and beans for dinner.

Dewdrop

Dewdrop spent a part of each day curiously moving from wagon to wagon searching for food and trying to make new friends, but she was most often met with shouts of "Get out of here!" or "Go away!" and seldom by a warm greeting. The day before departure was no different. At her first stop she raised up and placed her front paws on the back of a wagon to investigate the smell of food coming from inside and was immediately kicked to the ground by a gruff man unwilling to share his meal. Determined to find something to eat she continued to sniff her way along the train until she detected the scent of another dog coming from one of the wagons. When she raised up to see what was inside she found herself nose to nose with Angus. The two stared into each other's eyes long enough to determine that neither was a threat to the other.

Although it was a long way to the ground for Angus he jumped from the wagon and the two ran in circles around and under the wagon in a playful game of chase. It was the first opportunity for both to play with another dog in some time. Neva immediately noticed the commotion from a short distance away and, after making sure that the chase was a friendly one, allowed the two dogs to carry on until both were pooped. Dewdrop had managed to make a friend and got fed along with Angus as well. This was a wagon she would come back to.

A few of the wagons in the train were known as Conestoga Wagons. These were large, heavy wagons with curved floors rising up at each end to keep things from falling out when going up or down steep hills. They were designed to carry large amounts of cargo and had broad wheels for moving heavy loads through mud and over rough terrain. They carried the supplies that would be shared by all. Teams of eight or ten or even more animals were needed to pull these large wagons and moving them up steep trails and over mountains was difficult. For crossing deep rivers the wheels of a Conestoga could be removed so that the wagons became boats.

Almost all of the wagons in the train, however, were called Prairie Schooners. These were smaller, lighter wagons that could be pulled by smaller teams of animals. The overhead covers were made of white canvas stretched over wooden ribs. This made them look from a distance like the sailing ship known as a schooner. Some were designed and manufactured specifically to make the journey west, but many were farm wagons converted to covered wagons for the trip. They measured about eleven feet long and five feet wide. Although simple in appearance, these wagons included some technical features that were quite advanced. The design of the undercarriage, for example, included a kingpin which allowed the front wheels to pivot and front wheels that were smaller than the rear wheels. These features made turning and cornering much easier.

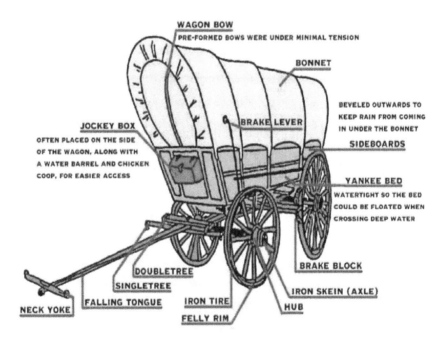

WAGON BOW
PRE-FORMED BOWS WERE UNDER MINIMAL TENSION

BONNET

BEVELED OUTWARDS TO
KEEP RAIN FROM COMING
IN UNDER THE BONNET

BRAKE LEVER

SIDEBOARDS

JOCKEY BOX
OFTEN PLACED ON THE SIDE
OF THE WAGON, ALONG WITH
A WATER BARREL AND CHICKEN
COOP, FOR EASIER ACCESS

YANKEE BED
WATERTIGHT SO THE BED
COULD BE FLOATED WHEN
CROSSING DEEP WATER

BRAKE BLOCK

DOUBLETREE
SINGLETREE
FALLING TONGUE   IRON TIRE
NECK YOKE
FELLY RIM

IRON SKEIN (AXLE)

HUB

Parts of a Prairie Schooner

Each wagon owner had to choose between horses, mules, and oxen to pull their wagon. Because horses could not live off the prairie grasses that grew along much of the trail and lacked the stamina to pull heavy wagons over long distances they were seldom used. The choice therefore came down to mules or oxen. Mules were strong, could survive on the prairie grasses, and were much faster than oxen, but were notoriously unruly and difficult to handle. Oxen were slower and required a "driver" to walk along beside them, but offered a number of advantages over mules. They not only could live on a diet of poor grasses, but possessed the greater strength needed to haul a heavy wagon up steep hills or drag it through deep mud, were better behaved and therefore more reliable, and were less expensive to buy. Oxen were also less likely to be stolen along the way. For these reasons, the majority of the wagons in the train would be pulled by teams of oxen and only a few by horses. The remaining horses would be those ridden by the men tending the livestock and those who could not afford a wagon and would attempt to make the journey only on horseback. Several cows would also start the journey. They would provide fresh milk and butter for their owners early in the trip and, if a lack of decent grasses or exhaustion prevented them from keeping up with the train, a steak dinner down the line.

It was easy to distinguish the wagons owned by wealthier emigrants from those owned by travelers who were forced to make compromises. The rich owned wagons that were larger, better built, and pulled by teams of six or more oxen. Their wagons were capable of carrying greater loads and things like tar buckets, water barrels, buckets of axle grease, extra axles and wheels, and coils of rope hung from the sides and back of these wagons. John Marshall owned such a wagon. Those with smaller wagons and teams of only two or four animals like that owned by Ryan and Neva Walsh simply prayed that the disparity would not be of practical importance on the trail.

A day before the train was scheduled to depart a large dog that looked to be a German Shepherd with a long, thick coat found its way into camp. He was tan and black in color, weighed well over a hundred pounds, and wore a leather collar on which the name "RAMBLES" was inscribed. He had a sad, but stately, appearance and bore the scars of many past skirmishes which suggested that his past had been a hard one.

Rambles

Rambles didn't belong to anyone on the train and was probably moving from one wagon camp to another looking for food. His presence in camp was reported to Captain Billy by several wagon owners with young children who were uncomfortable with the hungry look in Rambles' eyes. Billy tracked Rambles down, coaxed him to his side, and concluded from his gentle demeanor and his collar that he posed no threat to the campers. Billy had to decide, however, whether to let Rambles roam freely around the camp causing concern or whether it would be better to lead him into the woods and shoot him. Luckily, Rambles got close enough to Billy to lick him gently on the cheek and that made all the difference, even to a hardboiled old boy like Billy. Rambles was pardoned, but he didn't move on as Billy hoped he would. Instead he drifted off to hunt for food and then returned that night to sleep near Billy's campsite. Billy thought he would surely move on once the train left camp the next morning.

On the morning of departure everyone was busy maneuvering their wagons and teams into position in the pre-dawn darkness to await the official start of the journey. The wagons carrying Angus and Halo eventually came side to side and the two met for the first time. Neva was checking on her team one last time with Angus underfoot when Missy dropped Halo to the ground to see how the two dogs would react to each other. After a little introductory butt sniffing, it appeared that all would be well between them. Halo even rolled over on her back in a friendly gesture of submissiveness. The two would be seeing a lot of each other over the next several months.

Rambles was on his feet at the first sign of activity that morning and roamed among the wagons for some time before spotting Captain Billy eating breakfast with his lieutenants. The men allowed him to mooch a little bacon after which he sat patiently by Billy's side while Billy issued some last minute instructions. Rambles was more than ready to go even

14

though he had no idea where he was going or how long it would take to get there. It was almost an hour later when the sun began to peak through the trees, everyone and everything seemed ready to go, and Billy took his position at the head of the train. A moment later he fired a gunshot into the air and shouted as loud as he could, "Wagons Ho!" and the first wagon began to move. Dewdrop and the men driving the cattle would follow the last wagon onto the trail. The journey had begun.

CHAPTER 2 - STAMPEDE!

The much anticipated first day on the trail was exciting for everyone, but uneventful. The first part of the trip would cover the vast prairie grasslands that are now northeastern Kansas and Nebraska. Most of the emigrants walked alongside their wagons with their teams and their livestock rather than riding on the wagon seat. Some of the wagons had springs under the driver's seat and others did not, but there were none on the axles to cushion the bumps of trail ruts and rocks. The ride on the seat was therefore a rough one. Those who chose to ride on their wagon used blankets and other soft objects to soften the jarring blows to their behinds. A few were lucky enough to own a horse and rode it alongside their team. Halo and Angus walked along with their owners for most of the day, but their short legs could not quite cover the fifteen miles or so the train traveled each day and they usually ended up riding in their wagons for several hours at the end of the day. Captain Billy rode at the front of the train with Rambles either trotting alongside him or anxiously running ahead of the train to follow the fresh scents of animal teams pulling trains that had left Independence before them. Rambles' nose was turning out to be the train's best scout. Dewdrop walked with the cattle and their keepers expending only enough extra energy to keep any wanderers from drifting away from the herd.

Billy thought it was best to stop earlier in the day than did most of the other trail bosses in order to secure a good campsite. A good site is large and level and has clean, fresh water nearby, an ample supply of firewood, and good grasses for the livestock to eat. With many other trains seeking the same sites, those that pushed on until late in the day often had to set up camp in near darkness at a poor location. Billy felt that a good night's sleep was more important over the course of a two thousand mile walk across the country than the extra mile or two the train might have traveled each day.

Although many of the stopover points along the way were well known, it was always necessary to have one of the cattlemen ride ahead to make sure that preferred sites were not already occupied or to identify an acceptable alternative. Once a campsite was reached, Billy signaled as much to the others and the wagons formed a large, enclosed circle. The circle of wagons served both as a defensive compound and a corral for the more valuable livestock and animal teams. It provided protection against intrusions by Indian thieves, cattle rustlers, buffalo herds, and other unexpected threats. If the campsite was long and narrow, two smaller circles were formed. Because the wagons were always packed high and tight with food and supplies there was no room in them for the emigrants to sleep. Many slept in tents that they pitched just inside the wagon circle.

Others were not as well-equipped and slept directly on the ground under the stars. Physical exhaustion made sleeping easy even when the bed was a blanket on hard, lumpy ground.

Although each day was different in one way or another, the basic routine for all was well established. Everyone was awakened at about 5 a.m. to the sound of Captain Billy's trumpet, breakfast was prepared and eaten, the cattle that had been grazing overnight were rounded up, the tents and cooking utensils were packed up, and the animal teams were hitched to the wagons. The train was generally back on the trail before 7 a.m.

Breakfast was bacon, bread or biscuits, and coffee. Billy brought the train to a stop in the middle of each day for about an hour so that the emigrants could rest and eat a quick, cold lunch. Around 6 p.m. the train stopped again to set up camp for the night. After circling the wagons and tending to their animals, the campers would pitch their tents, start their campfires, and eat their dinners. Dinner for most consisted of bacon or whatever meat a local hunt produced, beans, rice, and coffee. After dinner some played cards or checkers, wrote letters, or mended clothing. Those with school aged children used this time to work with them on lessons they were missing while on the trail. This was also the time when any necessary wagon repairs were made. By 8 p.m. almost everyone was in bed.

Billy and the cowboys camped together in the open air and this brought Dewdrop and Rambles together as well. During the first few nights on the trail they got to know each other quite well and generally spent the nighttime hours sleeping only a short distance apart near the campfire. The cowboys fed them bacon for dinner, but never enough to fill their stomachs and they used the early evening hours to hunt for groundhogs and rabbits and anything else they could catch to eat. For these two there wasn't much of an opportunity to play after a long day on the trail. Angus and Halo, on the other hand, were more fortunate. Missy Marshall fed Halo and Neva Walsh fed Angus like the family members they were. They were small dogs and didn't require a lot of food.

Breaking Camp at Sunrise

(1858 painting by Alfred Jacob Miller)

The Marshall and Walsh wagons were always next to one another in the circle so it was always convenient for Halo, Angus, and Missy to play together each evening after dinner with no one having to leave their campsite. When it was time for bed, Neva placed Angus in a comfortable corner of the Walsh wagon for the night. Angus could leave the wagon at will, but needed a lift to get back into it. John and Emma Marshall slept in a tent, but a place in their wagon was cleared each night for Missy and Halo who slept cuddled together.

A few days into the trip the train passed the junction of the Oregon and Santa Fe trails. The Santa Fe Trail had been established almost thirty years earlier following Mexico's declaration of independence from Spain and was used to take traders from settlements in western Missouri southwest to the New Mexican capital of Santa Fe. Although none of the wagons in Captain Billy's train would leave to follow the Santa Fe Trail, as many as fifteen wagons made it known to Billy that they planned to leave the train near Fort Hall in what is now eastern Idaho and head south on the California Trail. This group intended to join the gold rush taking place in the mountains of California. Most of the wagons in Billy's train, however, were owned by people interested in farming and would remain with the train until it reached the fertile Willamette Valley in Oregon.

The very next day the train passed the first of many geologic landmarks it would come to along the way, the Blue Mound. Though it was hardly breathtaking, this long hump of earth rising out of the flat, grassy terrain which surrounded it made for a strange sight that was hard to miss.

It was only a few days into the trip before many of the emigrants realized that they had greatly overloaded their wagons and that the weight of the unnecessary items was already taking its toll on their animal teams making it difficult for them to keep up. This created gaps in the train that forced those in the rear to go faster and then slower instead of moving along at a steady pace. Those that overloaded had only one choice and that was to throw out the unneeded baggage. This was so common that it spawned a cottage industry in which opportunists came from various starting points in Missouri to fill wagons with the food, furniture, and other debris that littered the trail and then return to Independence to sell the goods to those just arriving.

During the first few weeks of the journey the train had to make a number of river crossings before reaching Fort Kearney, the first of several military outposts and resupply points it would pass along the trail. It would have to cross the Blue, the Wakarusa, the Kansas, the Vermillion, and the Big Blue rivers in what is now northeast Kansas and later the Little Blue River in what is now southeast Nebraska. River crossings were always dangerous and, if the rivers were deep and swift as they often were during the spring months, the high water often caused long delays.

The loss of supplies and deaths from drowning were not unusual at difficult crossings. It would later be reported that 37 people drowned crossing one river, the Green River in western Wyoming, in the year 1850 alone. Fortunately, water levels were unusually low at these early crossings and Billy's train was able to ford them all without having to unload the wagons to keep supplies dry or construct rafts to float the wagons across. Rambles and Dewdrop used these first crossings to take a long drink and a short bath and then leisurely walk or swim across the shallow waters. Angus and Halo both enjoyed a high and dry ride across the rivers in their wagons. Billy knew the train had been lucky up to this point and that more difficult crossings were yet to come.

On the eleventh day of the journey the train crossed the Big Blue River. It made the crossing late in the day without incident and stopped for the night on the western bank of the river. As the emigrants made camp they noticed that the sky had turned black well before sunset. It was apparent that a storm was about to begin, but before the travelers had time to prepare for it, the ominous clouds above produced a hard, soaking rain that immediately doused their campfires and sent everyone running for cover. Soon bolts of lightning were striking the ground nearby and the thunder that followed spooked the cattle and other livestock.

Dewdrop sensed the coming change in weather well before the storm began and pressed herself to the ground waiting to see what would happen next. She was already on high alert. With no natural protection anywhere around the campsite, the women and children sought shelter under or in their wagons while the men tried desperately to control the animals. Then, to make matters worse, the rain turned to hail. The hailstones grew larger and larger until some reached the size of apples. Now everyone was racing for cover of some kind. Those that hunkered down under wagons could hear but not see the damage the hail was doing to their wagon covers. Those sitting on piles of supplies inside their wagons covered their heads with pots and pans and watched in awe through an open end the incredible pounding the train was taking.

Halo and the Marshalls lay side by side on the ground under their wagon. Halo had been afraid of thunder since her days as a pup and, trembling uncontrollably, she burrowed hard into Missy's stomach in an effort to muffle the sound of the thunderclaps. Missy whispered into Halo's ear, "Don't be afraid dear girl, the thunder won't hurt you", but Missy was as worried as Halo and prayed that her words were the truth.

Neither Captain Billy nor any of the other trail veterans had ever seen anything like it. Billy's immediate concern was the safety of his steed, Bucket, but there was no time to think and little he could do. Billy quickly tied Bucket up tightly to one of the supply wagons and rolled under the wagon to protect himself. A confused Rambles was standing in the open when he heard Billy shout, "Come Rambles! Come under the wagon." That's all the encouragement Rambles needed and, without hesitating, he joined Billy under the wagon. Huddled there the two stared blankly at each other as if to ask, "What do we do now?" Billy finally confided, "Rambles old boy, in all my born days I don't believe I've ever been this low down", quite an admission from one who had spent countless nights sleeping on the ground.

Pelted by the hailstones, the terrified cattle became uncontrollable and began to stampede in an instinctive effort to escape the elements. The cowboys did their best to turn the herd, but they and their confused mounts were overwhelmed and unable to do much in the darkness but shield their heads from the hailstones. The stampeding cattle ran directly into and through the circled wagons knocking several over, trampling those sheltered beneath them, and scattering the panic-stricken horses, mules, and oxen within the circle. There was little Dewdrop could do to help until the storm began to subside. She followed the cattle some distance from the train, got ahead of them, and then managed to turn the leaders to the left and then to the left again. Her strategy was to have them run in circles rather that straight ahead until they became tired and stopped. A short time later the cowboys caught up with the herd and joined her in the roundup. Once they had the cattle settled down, Dewdrop ran off to locate the strays and return them one by one to the herd, a job that lasted well into the night. Only after her work was done did she feel the pain of the bruises caused by the hailstones.

Stampede in the Storm

(1908 painting by Frederic Remington)

It was just about midnight before the storm and the buzz among the emigrants that followed it died down. Captain Billy was looking for the only doctor traveling with the train, Dr. James Brookings. "Doc"

Brookings attended medical school in Philadelphia before moving west to St. Louis to establish his practice. Billy had met him in St. Louis after breaking his leg in a riding accident and was impressed not only with his medical skills, but with his youth and energy as well. Billy needed a doctor on the train and convinced Brookings in a series of letters to move his practice much farther west. Billy promised to make room in the common supply wagons for all of the medical equipment and supplies Brookings thought he might need on a trip of this kind and Brookings did not make any compromises. A large portion of his medical possessions ended up on the train. Brookings didn't wear a white shirt and black string tie as doctors of the day often did, but dressed and looked more like a cowboy than a doctor. He was an unmarried, good looking man of about thirty and would have been a prize catch for any single woman. This would be his first serious call to duty.

Billy and Doc Brookings worked their way around the train looking for injuries that required medical treatment. Anyone outside during the hailstorm had at least a few, if not many, cuts and bruises to show for it, but those with minor injuries could wait until daylight for treatment. As soon as word spread that Doc was looking for victims, a frantic couple ran up to him and pleaded for help. Their teenaged son was trampled in the stampede while trying to control his family's oxen team and was lying unconscious next to their wagon. Billy and Doc rushed to his side, but his injuries were so extensive that before the Doc could make a diagnosis and treat him he died. As difficult as it was to leave a mother and father so quickly after they had just lost their only son, Billy and Doc moved on to treat others who had also suffered serious injuries. Over the next few hours Doc set several broken bones and stitched up a number of bleeding wounds making good use of the splints, sutures, and other supplies he had brought along with him. On their walk back to the supply wagon Doc remarked to Billy in a low voice that no one else could hear, "It's a miracle that the injuries to those trampled when their wagons were overturned were not worse."

"You're right," Billy replied, "but I still have one to bury tomorrow. I hope it's the last".

It was not until sunup that the full impact of the storm could be determined. Everyone was busy gathering up belongings strewn about in the storm or locating missing tents, harnesses, and animal teams. Captain Billy and his officers went from wagon to wagon to assess the damage to each. Most of the damage to the wagons was to their covers and would cause no delay. Those who started the journey with thin or leaky covers found out as much the night before. Wet food and supplies were laid out to dry to avoid spoilage. A greater concern was the injuries to the animals that had to weather the storm unsheltered. Although it was fortunate that the teams pulling the wagons had been unhitched before the stampede began, several cattle, a mule and one horse were too badly injured to continue the journey and had to be shot. The Marshall's wagon was undamaged, but Ryan Walsh was not as lucky. "My wagon cover is in shreds," Ryan shouted over to John.

"No problem," responded John. "We'll be in Fort Kearny in a day or two and you can buy a new one there". It wouldn't be a problem Ryan thought if only I had the money to buy one.

Billy decided before daybreak that the train would not leave until the following day to allow everyone time to make any necessary repairs, enjoy a banquet of fresh beef, and catch up on the sleep they had lost the night before. Since there were no ministers or other clerics on the train, he would preside over the first funeral and burial of the trip. It was a somber affair attended by all but the seriously injured and a few cattlemen tending to the nervous herd. The boy was laid to rest in his grave wrapped in a sheet of burlap tied at both ends. A simple cross made of two small boards and bearing his name, age, and the date marked the gravesite. All four of the canines were there as well, sitting in two groups of two on opposite sides of the congregation watching, but not understanding, what was going on. Their reverence would be rewarded later that day with a huge meal of roasted mule and horsemeat that otherwise would have gone to waste.

For the next seven days the train would travel along the north bank of the Little Blue River, setting up camp each night at a location near the river. These were very good sites with water, wood, and fresh grasses readily available. This stretch of the Little Blue was home to one of the earliest native American tribes, the Pawnee. Longtime residents of the Great Plains and Platte River Basin, the Pawnee were primarily farmers, but left their farms during the summer and winter months to hunt buffalo.

The emigrants encountered several small groups of Pawnee during their travel along the Little Blue. To keep things cool, Captain Billy reminded everyone more than once that the Pawnee were known to be a friendly and "civilized" tribe that rarely had a dispute with white men. The Pawnee population numbered 20,000 or more before a smallpox epidemic in 1798 killed many of them and another in 1831 caused the death of almost half the tribe in a single winter. Diseases against which they had little natural resistance, the consumption of timber and grasses by those traveling along the Oregon Trail, and the disappearance of buffalo from their traditional hunting grounds decimated the Pawnee tribe during the 1840s and they were a beleaguered bunch by the time Billy's train passed through their territory. More of the same would eventually result in their elimination altogether from what is now the state of Nebraska.

It was along this easy stretch of trail that Rambles and Dewdrop had their first opportunities to socialize with Angus and Halo. Lying within earshot of the Walsh and Marshall wagons, the two larger dogs decided one evening to interrupt the play of Angus and Halo and introduce themselves. After engaging in some cautious butt sniffing, the four found no reason not to become friends. Missy was delighted that her pack had now expanded to four dogs and shouted to her mother, "Look, his collar says his name is Rambles! I wonder what the name of the other one is."

Rambles and Dewdrop were not much interested in the running games, but appreciated the affectionate pets and belly rubs Missy gave to all. This they did not get from Billy and the cowboys. Emma Marshall was less enthusiastic. She watched the group closely for some time to make sure the newcomers were no danger to Halo or Missy and finally spoke her thoughts aloud, "Missy, please don't expect me to feed those two big mouths."

Two days before reaching Fort Kearny, the train left the banks of the Little Blue and headed northwest toward the Platte River. It had been easy going since the night of the stampede and, although the bumps and bruises suffered in the storm were all but forgotten, the experience was not, particularly for those with serious injuries who were forced to ride in their wagons or those with wagon covers tattered beyond repair. Captain Billy discovered that all of the good campsites along this part of the trail had been occupied the night before and, because it was a Sunday, some trains were not traveling at all making the situation even more difficult. Since the train was still on schedule, Billy decided not to stop at midday as usual, but to call it quits as early in the afternoon as an acceptable site could be located. This would allow some extra time for those who were interested in holding prayer and Bible meetings. He thought to himself how useful having a minister along would have been and vowed not to leave Independence again without one.

CHAPTER 3 - LOST IN THE DESERT

Three weeks after leaving Independence the train arrived at Fort Kearny, a supply post on the Platte River established by the military just two years earlier. It was still relatively small and consisted only of two rows of wooden buildings facing each other with a parade ground in between. Although the fort was originally built to protect the growing number of emigrants from Indian attacks, it had no protective walls surrounding it and, up to this time, did not need any. It served instead as a safe resting place, message center, and resupply depot for those traveling west. The fort offered food for sale, fresh livestock in trade for tired or injured stock, and mail service to the east.

Once the fort came into view, an excited Rambles ran ahead and was the first to reach it. Captain Billy's scout had already informed him that the area around the fort was very crowded and that his train would have to camp either well short of the fort or well beyond it. He chose a site almost a mile beyond the fort so that his train could get ahead of others leaving at about the same time the next morning. In this way his passengers would endure only the dust of the wagons in front of them in his train, but avoid the heavier dust of other trains traveling ahead. It would also make securing a good campsite later in the day easier. Billy rode ahead to let the officers at the fort know the location of his campsite and when the train would break camp to hit the trail. This was necessary to avoid the conflicts that often arose when two or more trains tried to leave at the same time. Because his campsite and departure time were well chosen Billy was granted his "reservation".

Fort Kearny Circa 1850

(Undated painting by William Henry Jackson)

By the time Billy's train reached the fort Rambles had already seen it all and rejoined the train as it passed by. The train's arrival in midafternoon allowed plenty of time for those needing to buy food or supplies, trade injured animals for fresh ones, or replace livestock lost in the storm to return to the fort and take care of business. There was also time for those with the energy to do so to trade stories with emigrants from other trains camped nearby and to share information acquired from traders and soldiers traveling eastbound on the trail.

As the campers set up for the night, John Marshall noticed that Ryan Walsh did not intend to go back to the fort with the others and inquired, "Ryan, what about the new cover for your wagon?" Ryan reluctantly admitted that he didn't want to spend so much of the little money he had so early in the trip. John reminded him that a heavy rain would cost him as much in ruined supplies and made Ryan an offer that Ryan would have liked to refuse, but did not.

"I'll loan you the money for a cover and you can pay me back once you get your feet on the ground in Oregon," John said. Ryan thanked John and quickly turned away to hide the tear or two of gratitude running down his cheek.

After the shoppers returned from the fort and everyone had finished their dinners, the camp quieted down quickly. This was about the time when all of the dogs would congregate near the Marshall wagon for what was becoming a nightly rendezvous. Under the watchful eye of her mother, Missy was knee deep in fur when she said, "Mother, I asked around and found out the name of the other dog. It's Dewdrop!" The evening activity at the Marshall wagon was attracting the interest of other children on the train and it was not long before one or more were joining the gathering.

"What do you think, John?" Emma asked her husband.

"The dogs seem ok. I hear the two big ones are quite helpful," he replied. As dusk became darkness Emma called Missy and Halo to bed and Dewdrop and Rambles drifted wearily off to their usual sleeping grounds to rest up for the next day's march.

Captain Billy had spread the word that the train needed to get an early start the next day and sounded the morning wakeup call a little earlier than usual. From Fort Kearny the train would travel along the south shore of the Platte River for nearly 330 miles through the Great Plains, an area of rolling prairie and lush grasses that extends hundreds of miles across the central part of what is now the state of Nebraska. With no trees or shrubs anywhere in sight for days on end, this endless sea of lush grasses and fragrant wildflowers was a thing of beauty that emigrants from the east had never seen before.

The first days of travel along the Platte River were easy ones. The river was almost a half mile wide in places and small islands were everywhere, but it was slow moving and only a few feet deep most of the time. It was fortunate that the train would not to have to cross it until it split into the North and the South branches as the banks were soft and sandy and would support very little weight. Ryan Walsh had another use for the rivers along which the train would travel and that was to fish in them. He was not much of a hunter, but spent a good part of his youth fishing for trout and salmon in his native Ireland. The string and hooks

33

needed to get the job done weighed almost nothing and took up no room at all compared to the guns and ammunition required to supplement one's food supply by hunting.

Campsite by the Riverside

(1871 painting by Albert Bierstadt)

After nearly a month on the trail, Ryan decided it was time to find out if his angling skills were still sharp. He hastily unhitched and secured his team and set up camp for the night before anxiously heading for the Platte with Neva and Angus following close behind. Ryan tied a generous length of string to the end of a stiff, five foot long tree branch he had fashioned into a fishing pole early in the trip, tied a hook to the other end of the string, and baited the hook with a fat and lively earthworm. It was

Neva's job to overturn rocks along the river bank and collect the wriggling creatures that lived under them in a can she carried along for just that purpose. "Well Neva, here we go", Ryan said as he swung his bait into a likely looking hole six feet or so from the river's edge. Almost at once the line went taught and, with a sharp jerk of his pole, Ryan had his first fish on. Angus was watching the action intently and, excited by the silvery flashes of the struggling fish, jumped into the water in an attempt to catch it a second time.

This little scene was replayed half a dozen times as the trio moved along the river bank before Ryan offered Neva a promotion from worm catcher to fisherman. After a few poorly timed misses, she caught one, then another, and then another. "This is fun! Can we do it again tomorrow?" she asked.

As Ryan strung up their catch for the short walk back to camp, he replied, "Sure enough," just to make her happy. He then added with a puzzled look on his face, "Neva, I think we're a fish short". An impatient Angus wasn't waiting to eat with the others and had helped himself to an early dinner when no one was looking. Eyeing the partial remains of the missing fish Ryan laughed and said, "Angus my friend, that's the one you won't get later!" That night the Walshes and their delighted guests, the Marshalls, enjoyed a sumptuous fresh fish dinner, a welcome change from bacon, bacon, and more bacon. The Walsh fish fry would become a frequent event from that evening on.

Although much of the annual rainfall on the plains occurs in the summer months, the weather was fair and the trail dry for five days after leaving Fort Kearny before the train came to a muddy stretch of trail that was all but impassable. It had obviously rained hard in this area the night before and the wagons and the teams pulling them were sinking a foot or more into the muck requiring frequent and time consuming "rescues". As a result, the train was forced to weave its way around the soft spots following a course set by Billy and one of the cowboys riding ahead and probing the turf as they went. This slowed the train to a crawl and, after several days of good progress, it had traveled less than five miles along the muddy trail before it was time to stop again for the night.

The following morning Doc Brookings was called to the wagon of a family of three that had become sick in the night. A young girl of about six was lying on a blanket on the ground next to her mother when he arrived. Both were trembling and sweating profusely. After just a minute or two Doc asked, "What have you been eating?" The girl's father told Doc that his wife and daughter drank the milk of their cow every day and that they all ate butter made from the milk as well. After ruling out the diseases that most commonly show up on the trail, Doc concluded that the family had been poisoned by their cow's milk after it had eaten poisonous weeds the previous day. "I think the milk was bad," Doc told the man.

"That makes sense. I thought that cow was acting funny," replied the father.

Doc told the man, "All I can do for your wife and daughter now is keep them hydrated and pray that their symptoms pass. You must decide if your family is well enough to travel in your wagon when the train leaves in an hour or if you need to stay behind and join up with another train as it passes. If you decide to move out with us, I'll find someone to manage your team until you are well enough to do it yourself."

It wasn't much of a choice and the man quickly answered, "We'll be leavin' with you Doc, but first I've got to shoot that cow." Doc was not optimistic about their chances for recovery, but the condition of the two women had improved somewhat by the end of the day and, after a second day of misery, the two were obviously on a path to recovery.

The next morning the train crossed the south branch of the Platte River without incident and by the end of the day had reached Ash Hollow, a beautiful, wooded canyon and a welcome relief for the tired travelers struggling their way down Windlass Hill to the oasis below. Clean, sweet, spring water and ample firewood made Ash Hollow a popular stopover point and Billy's train found an ideal campsite along the south bank of the North Platte. As the train traveled west from Ash Hollow, however, the trail became increasingly dry and dusty, the green grasses gradually turning to brown and then disappearing completely. With no shade to be found, the arid stretch of desert ahead would be the most difficult test of stamina and temperament for both man and beast that the emigrants had encountered so far.

During the noon break the next day, Halo was resting in the shade under the Marshall's wagon, ignoring the clouds of dust circulating at ground level and peering out at the landscape through the spokes of the wheels when she spotted a rabbit, the first she had seen in some time. Yielding to her natural instincts, the temptation of a chase was just too much to resist. She sprang to her feet and took off after the rabbit as fast as she could. Halo must have gotten between the rabbit and its burrow because it never did disappear into the safety of a hole to end the chase as she had expected.

Operating on its home turf, the rabbit was a sure bet to outlast the small dog in the intense heat, but Halo's persistence was admirable. She continued her pursuit for nearly fifteen minutes, pausing to catch her breath only when the rabbit, comfortable with its large lead, stopped to reassess the danger. Finally, she became too pooped to go on and, panting uncontrollably, gave up the chase. From her resting place she looked around for the rabbit, but it was nowhere to be seen and neither was the train. Halo was so focused on her prey that she had no idea if, or how many times, she had changed direction during the chase and wondered now in which direction she should go to get back. Although the terrain was not featureless, the desert floor was all she saw in her excitement. She tried to pick up her own scent, but the hot, dry path she had traveled was not one she was able to retrace by nose. She wandered around for some time, barking at times in the hope that someone would hear her, and then sat down, overheated and exhausted, unable to go on and not sure what to do next.

Captain Billy had already given the signal to move out before Missy realized that Halo was missing. The Marshall wagon was near the front of the train and had to move ahead or out the way without delay. Missy was frantically running in all directions calling out Halo's name when John Marshall told her they could wait no longer and had to leave. In tears Missy pleaded with her father, "Please pull aside and wait until we find Halo." He thought for a minute and agreed to let the rest of the train pass so he could check to make sure that Halo was not somewhere among the wagons behind them.

As each wagon passed John asked, "Have you seen a small brown dog anywhere around?" No one had.

The cattle were the last to pass and, after John quickly explained the situation to the cowboys riding with them, the lead cowboy named Jesse was touched by the sight of Missy sobbing as she gripped her mother's hand. He said to John, "I think they can do without me for a while. I'll look for your dog for an hour or so and then that's it. It's too hot to be out there much longer." John thanked him and moved his wagon into line at the back of the train. Jesse knew he didn't have much of a chance of finding Halo without help and shouted out to the shepherd trotting along nearby, "Dewdrop! Come girl. I've got a job for you."

The search party of two followed John's wagon to the spot where it sat when Halo went missing and then broke off in the direction Jesse believed Halo most likely had taken. They moved in what appeared to be random circles, but it was more of an ever expanding spiral that, hopefully, would cross Halo's trail at some point. The scents of the local desert inhabitants kept Dewdrop busy, but she seemed to know that they were not what she was looking for.

The search was well over an hour old and Jesse was about to give it up when Dewdrop drifted off in a straight line seemingly with a purpose. The heat was oppressive, but it would be no cooler riding with the cattle and, because Dewdrop was moving in the same direction as the train was traveling, Jesse decided to continue the search a while longer. It was fortunate that Dewdrop was familiar with Halo's scent from their evenings together and now that she had finally found it her pace quickened. Jesse noticed the change and continued to follow her even though the search had now gone on much longer than planned.

At the same time Halo was desperately trying to find her way back, but her short, panicky bursts this way and that were not helpful. Confused and exhausted, the little dog wandered aimlessly for another hour before deciding to rest again. As the sun moved lower in the sky, she found some shade behind a large rock and laid down there to wait. It was all she could do.

Dewdrop was becoming increasingly excited and, moving along still faster, began to bark as if to offer encouragement to Jesse. It was only a few minutes later that Dewdrop heard a faint answer to her barking and, after exchanging barks a few more times, Dewdrop led Jesse directly to Halo's resting place. Jesse stepped off his horse, picked Halo up, and thought to himself that the odds of actually finding her in this wasteland would put it in the category of a miracle. Jesse and the dogs had a long drink of water from his canteen and a short rest before beginning the ride back, a relieved Halo riding high under Jesse's left arm.

Jesse and Dewdrop didn't catch up with the train before it had stopped for the day and the sky was nearly dark. A forlorn Missy was lying awake alone in her bed thinking about Halo when she heard Jesse and John talking outside the wagon. "That was a long hour or so, Jesse," she heard her father say. She assumed the worst, but her tears of sorrow quickly turned to tears of joys when she heard Halo's high pitched bark a moment later.

Jesse quickly told the tale of the search and finished it with the statement, "If it wasn't for Dewdrop, your dog would still be out there." As a small reward for a huge debt of gratitude Emma insisted that Jesse and, of course, Dewdrop, stay for a very special late dinner. Tired, but hungry, they graciously accepted. With Halo in her arms Missy said her prayers for a second time that night, thanking God for answering her first. As the two drifted off to sleep Missy wondered how she could ever repay Dewdrop for her good deed.

On the 38th day of the trip the train made camp near a closely spaced pair of guiding landmarks known as Court House Rock and Jail Rock. These were massive sandstone structures that rose well over 200 feet above their bases. At an elevation of more than 4000 feet above sea level the rocks could be seen from the east as far as forty miles or three days travel away.

Only twelve miles farther west the train passed perhaps the best known landmark along the entire trail, Chimney Rock, a sharply pointed, cone-shaped rock composed of Brule clay and sandstone. Standing almost 300 feet high it was a strange and magnificent sight that could be seen from many miles away to the east. Captain Billy halted the train a little earlier in the day than he normally did to allow everyone to enjoy a relaxed view of the imposing rock from a campsite close to its base. Chimney Rock marked the end of the trek across the prairies and the beginning of a steeper and more rugged climb toward the Rocky Mountains.

Chimney Rock

CHAPTER 4 - RAMBLES AND RATTLERS

It was late May when the train left its campsite at the base of Chimney Rock and headed northwest toward Robidoux Pass, the pass over which the train would cross through the Wildcat Hills. The monotony of the landscape and the hot, dry, dusty conditions along this stretch of trail led to levels of boredom and fatigue that tested the patience of all. The topography of the trail, however, made it possible for the wagons to travel side by side sometimes four or five abreast so that those traveling in the rear of the train had to breathe less of the dust kicked up by the wagons ahead. The emigrants also began to notice an increasing number of graves scattered along the south bank of Platte River and the thoughts of those lying in the graves further contributed to the tension and uneasiness among them. Then, to make matters worse, word of a cholera outbreak quickly spread throughout the train.

Only hours after leaving Chimney Rock, Doc Brookings reported to Captain Billy that a family of four had contracted cholera, presumably from drinking infected water from the same source. Cholera was a fast moving disease and death or signs of a recovery usually occurred within the first twenty four hours. Outbreaks on the trail were part of a worldwide pandemic that began in Asia and later spread to cities throughout the United States. The disease peaked along the trail during the years 1849-1850 at the height of the California gold rush when traffic on the trail was heavy and unsanitary conditions were common.

Once the train had made camp for the night, Brookings and two women from neighboring wagons were doing their best to make the victims comfortable, but without a known cure for the disease all Doc could do was try to control their symptoms. He confided to Billy later that night, "I don't think these folks are going to make it. I'd plan around a funeral tomorrow". All were dead by morning. Mercifully, their suffering was short-lived and their case appeared to be an isolated one, although Billy was not willing to announce that to the others just yet.

Burials on the trail were problematic. Many were decent affairs, but as the trip wore on the sick were often abandoned to die alone or hastily buried in shallow graves that were easily dug up by animals in search of a meal. In some cases a "watcher" was left behind to remain with the sick until death occurred. Graves were dug while the watcher waited and burials were sometimes a bit premature to save time. Historians would later estimate that the average distance between graves from Independence to Oregon City was only fifty yards. Captain Billy resolved to treat the sick and dying on his train with compassion and respect unless, of course, things got really bad. With a number of volunteers working under Billy's supervision, the unfortunate family were buried later that morning in deep and properly marked graves. The train was several hours late leaving camp that day.

A Death on the Trail

On the 41st day of the trip the train approached Robidoux Pass and the emigrants got their first glimpse of the Rocky Mountains far to the west. Named for a Frenchman who established a trading post a few years earlier on the east side of the pass, Robidoux Pass was used by all who traveled the trail until Mitchell Pass, located nine miles to the north near Scott's Bluff, was opened a year later in 1851. It then became the primary route for travelers, cutting eight miles from the route of the original trail.

Spring water and firewood were plentiful on the east side of Robidoux Pass and any needed supplies could be bought at the trading post. These amenities made the site a popular stopover point. Prices for goods purchased on the trail were generally much higher, however, than those paid in Independence for the same things. Flour, for example, sold for as much as a dollar per pint on the trail as compared to $4.00 a barrel in Independence. Sugar and coffee also fetched very high prices. The exception was bacon. Most westbound travelers left Independence with a lot of bacon on board and a price of a penny a pound on the trail was not uncommon. Excess bacon was often dumped along the trail to lighten a wagon's load. This was particularly good news for the dogs as few, if any, of the emigrants thought twice about sharing their supply of bacon with them.

High prices on the trail, however, worked in favor of those with excess supplies. Any unneeded items could be sold at good prices or traded for things that had greater value than they were worth in Independence, a convenient alternative to discarding them along the trail. The traffic on the trail in 1850 made it a good time to be a seller.

The next morning the train began its ascent to the summit of the pass, a relatively easy climb compared to those yet to come. From the summit the travelers could clearly see Scott's Bluff, a huge rock formation which would later become an important waypoint for those taking the shorter route through Mitchell's Pass to the north. Once over the summit, the train continued to follow the North Platte River toward what is now the Wyoming border and then on to Fort Laramie. Four long, but uneventful, days later the train reached the fort.

Fort Laramie, located at the confluence of the North Platte and Laramie Rivers, was founded in the 1830s to service the fur traders traveling in both directions. It later became the most significant center of economic activity in the region and a primary stopping point for those traveling on the Oregon Trail. In 1949, a year earlier, the site was converted by the U. S. Army to a military fort for the purpose of protecting emigrants against Indian attacks although such attacks were still rare at this time. As many as 350,000 travelers stopped at Fort Laramie over the course of the migration west. Billy again chose a campsite on the far side of the fort in order to be the first train on the trail the next day.

Fort Laramie

(1937 sketch by Alfred Jacob Miller)

That evening some of the emigrants did a little shopping, the cowboys did a little drinking, and the dogs each went their own way for a change. Angus and the Walshes went fishing, Halo and the Marshalls walked to the fort to check it out and pick up a few supplies, and Dewdrop hung out with the cowboys. Rambles was dozing contentedly in the flickering light of Captain Billy's campfire, digesting an unusually sumptuous dinner of bacon, beans, and bread. Billy was in a generous mood that night as he worked out his plan for the days ahead.

Between Fort Laramie and the point at which the train would finally have to cross the North Platte, a number of tributaries feeding the main river from the south had to be crossed. The Laramie River was the first, followed by crossings of the Horse, Cottonwood, La Bonte, Bad Tick, La Prele, Deer and Box Elder Creeks among others. These crossings were not particularly difficult, but every crossing had to be undertaken with preparation and care and even minor crossings might take as much as half a day. As a result, this leg of the journey took almost a full week to complete.

After leaving Fort Laramie the train crossed the Laramie River, continued to follow the southern shore of the North Platte, and stopped that first night in the shadow of Register Cliff, a prominent landmark rising 100 feet above the valley floor. The emigrants used it as a message board, etching their name, the date, their home city and, if time permitted, a short message into the soft limestone formation. Many of the inscriptions can still be read today. Billy's train made camp early enough in the day to allow time for those interested in reading the inscriptions of earlier emigrants and chiseling their names into the wall of the cliff to do so. Register Cliff was the first of three such locations along the trail where the emigrants would have an opportunity to record their passage.

The Marshalls were among those making the short hike to the cliff to add their names with Halo and Angus anxiously leading the way. After reading a number of the carvings Missy remarked, "Father, a lot of other people from Ohio have already been here."

John was preoccupied, working hard on his inscription which included the names of Emma and Missy and, after stepping back to admire it, replied, "Well, now there's three more".

Missy read his carving and asked with a disappointed look on her face, "Where's Halo's name?"

John just rolled his eyes and said to Emma, "Let's get back for dinner. I'm hungry."

Dewdrop and Rambles were sitting with the cowboys waiting for their dinner handout and watching the emigrants coming and going when Dewdrop decided to investigate the activity at the cliff more closely. She planned to do a little hunting at the same time and so headed well off the path taken by the others to an area that had not yet been disturbed. She stuck her nose into every hole in the ground and every crack and crevice in the rocks that might be home to something to eat, but detected nothing. With very little daylight remaining she was about to give up the hunt when she saw movement in an opening under a large rock. She instinctively froze for a moment and then began a slow stalk toward the opening. To Dewdrop's surprise whatever was moving under the rock did not retreat even though she was now only a few feet away. She then heard a rattling sound unfamiliar to her and attempted to back off, but before she could do so, she heard the same sound coming from behind her. She had aroused a den of rattlesnakes and was now trapped between two that were coiled for action. Others were slithering out of the den to join the fray. She thought that some aggressive growling and barking might intimidate the snakes, but this proved to be an ineffective defense. The snakes gave no ground and rattled even louder.

Just when Dewdrop thought something had to happen, Rambles burst onto the scene in a full run, grabbed one of the snakes, and shook it as hard as he could. He had heard Dewdrop's barking from his resting place nearly a hundred yards away and immediately sensed that she was in trouble. Dewdrop used the diversion to flee to safety a short distance away before turning back to watch Rambles and the snakes finish their short engagement. Rambles had killed one of the snakes with a hard bite to the head, but it was hardly a victory. He had been bitten twice in the skirmish before joining Dewdrop beyond the striking distance of the surviving snakes.

By the time Dewdrop and Rambles got back to the cowboys' campsite, Rambles was in considerable distress and his face, now badly swollen, was barely recognizable. Panting and drooling uncontrollably, he pawed continuously at his wounds in a vain effort to erase them. Jesse immediately diagnosed his condition. "This dog's been snakebit!" he proclaimed and told one of the cowboys to go for Doc Brookings.

By the time Brookings arrived Rambles had sunk to the ground and was having difficulty breathing. Although his thick coat made the exam difficult, Brookings located the two bites and told Jesse and the others, "I don't know if he'll make it, but at least the bites are on his face and leg. Body bites would have been much worse." Doc went on to explain that Rambles' chances also depended on the amount of venom he had received which, in turn, depended on the size of the snakes that bit him and how long it had been beforehand that the snakes had bitten anything else. He finished up by saying, "He's a big dog. Let's hope they were small snakes."

Captain Billy was eventually called to the scene and, after hearing Doc's report, said, "Well, I would have shot him and left him to the buzzards a few months ago, but he's since earned the right to die or recover on his own. Either way, he's in no shape to lead our parade come morning. What should we do?" These were the days long before a venom antidote had been developed. Doc instructed Billy to keep him from moving around, give him plenty of water, and check on him frequently to make sure the swelling didn't choke him to death. Doc and Billy slid Rambles onto a blanket and carried him to a hastily prepared "recovery" room directly behind the bench seat of one of the common supply wagons. Later that night Billy recruited a teenaged boy named Jacob Miller who had no daytime duties to ride on the supply wagon with Rambles in order to keep a close eye on him.

Rambles was bitten by Prairie Rattlesnakes, a species found over much of the Great Plains east of the Rockies. Living primarily on small animals like rats, mice, squirrels, rabbits and prairie dogs, these snakes will eat birds, lizards, and other snakes as well. In the summer months they hunt by night, remaining in their dens the during daylight hours to avoid the heat. The Prairie Rattler is not a particularly large snake and, although their venom glands are small, its venom is potent. It is capable of delivering a lethal bite to an adult human although deaths from Prairie Rattlesnake bites are rare.

Before the train left Register Cliff the next morning, Captain Billy checked to make sure Rambles was still alive. He was and though he looked bad, he didn't seem any worse than he did the night before. Billy instructed Jacob to let him know if there was any change in his condition and left the two to get the train moving. Jacob was enthusiastic about his assignment as Rambles' caretaker as it provided a welcome relief from the boredom of the long daily walk alongside his wagon. There was little in a practical way that Jacob could do for him, but his watchful eye and gentle stroking of Rambles' back and belly afforded Rambles some comfort.

Word of Rambles' condition circulated quickly among those traveling in the forward part of the train and by the time it had stopped for the midday rest visitors were lined up to see how Rambles was doing. Missy and Halo were there well before the entire train had stopped. Billy and Jesse showed up a few minutes later with Dewdrop tagging along and Doc Brookings arrived shortly after that. Jacob gave each a detailed account of Rambles' condition and summarized his report by saying "He's no better, but no worse."

Doc Brookings concluded that the period of greatest danger had passed, but in case he was wrong whispered only to Billy, "I think he's going to be ok." Dewdrop sat nearby knowing only that Rambles was somewhere in the wagon. She couldn't appreciate Rambles' fight for life, but she did understand his role in her escape.

When the train stopped for the day, Captain Billy's check on Rambles found him looking much the same, but his breathing was less labored and he was drinking some water. He had no interest, however, in the bacon dinner Billy had brought along for him. Billy told Jacob to return to his family and report for duty again the next morning. Billy would maintain the vigil until then by sleeping next to Rambles' recovery wagon.

Over the next few days, the plains over which the train had traveled for weeks gradually turned mountainous, marking the point where emigrants were forced to ease the burden on their teams by further lightening their loads, abandoning any heavy or unnecessary items along the trail. After making a first cut, those that were still overstocked would soon be pitching out some of their bacon and other foodstuffs as well. In places the trail became a rut in the limestone created by the passage of earlier wagons. Over time thousands of wagon wheels produced depressions in the limestone sections of the trail that were several feet deep. These ruts can still be seen today.

It would be six days before Rambles was well enough to again travel with Captain Billy at the head of the train. For several days preceding his return to duty, he used both the midday break and the evening stopovers to roam around outside the wagon, making up for the meals he had missed, doing his business, and regaining his strength. Rambles was more than ready to leave the confinement of the wagon permanently when the train stopped to camp for the night on Day 52, the day before the North Platte River crossing. Billy thanked Jacob for his service and, as his reward, told him "Son, you get to ride my horse at the front of the train the day after we cross the river. I'll walk with the oxen pulling the supply wagon." Jacob was speechless, but his wide open eyes and broad smile did the talking for him.

Wagon Ruts in the Limestone Trail

Captain Billy and his staff met for some time that night to decide just how to cross the river. The crossing was planned at the location most often used by Oregon Trail travelers, a site close to what is presently the city of Casper, Wyoming. The first toll bridge at this crossing was not built until 1853, but there was one commercial ferry in service at the time. Known as The Mormon Ferry, it was established by members of the Church of Latter-Day Saints a few years earlier, moved four miles downstream in 1849, and operated by church members each emigration season until competing ferries and toll bridges forced it to close in 1853. The fee was $1.50 to $5.00 per crossing depending on the condition of the river.

The North Platte was perhaps a hundred and fifty yards wide at the point where the crossing was to take place and, unlike earlier crossings, the water was running fast and deep due to the spring runoff. The main channel meandered from one side of the river to the other and the bottom was a mix of shifting sandbars and mud. If a path shallow enough to ford the river could be found, supporting the weight of the wagons could be a problem and any wagon unable to keep moving might have the loose sand under its wheels washed out by the current, sinking it hopelessly into the quicksand.

Another option would be to convert the wagons to small boats by removing the wheels and dismantling the undercarriage, making the wagon box watertight with tar, and then ferrying everything across in these "boats", either by towing them with man or animal power or by rowing or poling them across.

A third alternative would be to swim most of the animals over, build large canoes by hollowing out cottonwood logs, lash the canoes together into a raft, and then float the wagons, supplies, and people over on the rafts. Since the river conditions were unfavorable, the wagons would have to be unpacked and ferried over separately from their contents. If rafting the river was chosen as the crossing method, stringing a cable across the river between trees on each side to keep the rafts from moving too far downstream with the current would also be necessary. The train could also wait on the south side of the river until the water level dropped and the current subsided, but there was no way of knowing how long the wait might be or if fording the muddy, sandy bottom after the wait would be any easier than rafting across.

No one thought that waiting was a good idea. Rafting the wagons and supplies across separately would be the safest, but most time-consuming of the alternatives. Everyone agreed, however, that attempting to ford the river at this time would be much too dangerous and so decided on a mix of the other options. The plan was to swim all of the animals except those needed to move the wagons onto the rafts across first, build the rafts needed to ferry those unwilling to pay the $5.00 toll or who carried no tar to seal their wagons, and allow the others to either utilize the Mormon Ferry service or to convert their wagons to boats. The crossing would take two full days to complete if nothing went wrong.

The next day Jesse and the cowboys swam the cattle and wagon teams across the river in manageable groups and strung the cable, the boys and men built the rafts, and the women organized their wagons to efficiently unload the contents onto the rafts and then quickly reload them onto their wagons on the other side. This would be no small task as the supplies carried by each wagon weighed as a much as a ton. The contents of each wagon would cross first so that the reloading process could take place as soon as the owner's wagon arrived at the far side.

It was an off day for the children and all of the dogs except Dewdrop. She made the crossing more than once, wading where she could and swimming with the livestock where she couldn't. Miraculously, not a single animal was lost in the crossing, although a few were swept as much as fifty yards downstream by the current before reaching the far shoreline. Once all of the livestock were safely across and back in the pack, Dewdrop dropped to the ground, exhausted. She spent that evening resting and dining with the cowboys on the far side of the river. Angus and Halo passed the day playing with Missy, studying the preparation activities, and splashing around in a shallow pool near the water's edge to cool off and drink more of the cold, fresh water than they could hold. Between naps Rambles wandered among the wagons with Captain Billy hoping for a handout or two.

Early the following morning supplies and wagons began moving across the river on the newly constructed rafts. The Marshalls and their wagon crossed on the Mormon Ferry to spare Emma and Missy the burden of unloading and loading their large, well-stocked wagon. John also felt that the size and stability of the commercial ferry offered safer passage for his possessions than did hastily constructed rafts. The ferry ride saved John no work, however, as he toiled longer and harder than most on the construction of the rafts. Halo and Missy made the crossing in the safety of their nest inside the Marshall wagon. Captain Billy also decided to use the Mormon Ferry to carry the common supply wagons across as these were very large and extremely heavy wagons. The few who used the ferry did so only for their loaded wagons. Their animal teams and other livestock swam with the others to minimize the cost of the crossing. Dewdrop and the cowboys spent crossing day watering the livestock and sorting out the animal teams by wagon owner to save time when the train was otherwise ready to go.

Rafting Across the North Platte River

(1949 drawing by unknown artist)

Angus made the crossing with Neva and the Walsh's supplies. Sitting proudly atop the Walsh pile of belongings, one of two stacked on the raft, he looked like a miniature pirate after a bloody victory. Ryan and the Walsh wagon were not far behind on a second raft. Captain Billy remained on the near side of the river the entire day supervising the operation until the last wagon had been loaded onto a raft. Unsure if Rambles had the stamina to swim the river so soon after his recovery, Billy put him on the last raft to make the crossing. Astride his horse, Billy followed closely behind. By the time everyone and everything had reached the north side of the river, it was almost dark. The men acting as raft operators had gone back and forth across the river many times during the course of the day and the unloading and reloading of the wagons took its toll on everyone else. Needless to say, it was not difficult for most to fall asleep that night.

CHAPTER 5 - RUSTLERS IN THE NIGHT

It was early June when the train left its campsite the morning after the North Platte crossing. Captain Billy made good on his promise to Jacob and, as Jacob proudly mounted Bucket, Billy said to him, "Don't get too far ahead and keep your eye on Rambles. I'll be right behind you." Billy knew the trail ahead was an easy one to follow and that Bucket knew the drill well enough to keep Jacob in check.

Before signaling the train to move out, Billy instructed Jesse to remain at the campsite and wait for the next train or two to arrive at the crossing in order to sell the rafts his train had built. After all, the rafts would save the next train at least one travel day and a lot of hard work. The buyers could then resell them to the next train to come along and so on. He figured they might fetch enough to cover the Mormon Ferry rides that were paid from the common fund in which all on the train had a share. Billy also suggested to Jesse that he offer the rafts to the Mormons since their business would be hurt by a string of buyers. Either way, it was up to Jesse's to negotiate the best deal he could.

After completing the North Platte River crossing, the train did not see it again for almost three days as the trail followed a more northerly route away from the river. Late in the morning of third day, the train reached the point where a tributary of the North Platte, the Sweetwater River, and the trail came together. From this point, the train would travel along the Sweetwater for over 200 miles to its headwaters near South Pass and the Continental Divide. This stretch of trail was common to all three of the trails leading west, the Oregon Trail, the California Trail which took travelers to the gold country of northern California, and the Mormon Trail on which Mormons stopping in northern Utah and those headed all the way to southern California traveled. For this reason, traffic along the Sweetwater was heavy.

Late on that third day, the train approached perhaps the most noted waypoint west of Fort Laramie known as Independence Rock. This huge piece of granite is 1900 feet long, 850 feet wide, and stands 130 feet above its base. The emigrants were divided on whether the rock looked more like a whale or a turtle. Many of them stopped to carve their names into it, but found it far more difficult to make a mark in the hard rock than in the soft limestone of Register Cliff and most ended up painting their message on the rock in pine tar. It was late afternoon when Captain Billy called the train to a halt and circled the wagons in an open area in the shadow of the rock. The abundance of good grasses close to the rock made it a popular stopover point and Billy hoped that no other trains would arrive at the site before the day ended. None did.

Circling the Wagons for the Night

(1880 painting by C. A. A. Christensen)

After everyone had eaten that night, Missy Marshall and Halo went from wagon to wagon carrying her mother's cookpot to collect leftovers and discards to supplement Dewdrop's meager dinner with the cowboys. By this time practically everyone on the train knew all of the dogs by name as well as the story of Dewdrop's role in finding Halo in the desert. The dinner pot was one of the ways Missy had thought of to repay Dewdrop for her good work. "Passing the pot for Dewdrop" was Missy's short, but effective pitch. Not everyone added something to the pot, but enough did to provide a substantial mix of things to eat. Missy made the short walk to the cowboy's campfire and asked Jesse where Dewdrop could be found.

Jesse had to call Dewdrop's name only once to bring her running to the fire. Studying the contents of the pot, Jesse laughingly said to the others, "This looks a whole lot better than the stuff we just ate!" The cowboys all agreed. Dewdrop didn't need a formal invitation to gobble down Missy's offering and, after licking the pot clean, gave Missy a satisfied look of appreciation.

As soon as Dewdrop had finished, Missy left by saying, "We've got to go now. My mother will be worried about her pot", and she and Halo ran off to squeeze in a little playtime with Angus before bedtime.

Travel along the Sweetwater was a welcome relief from the dry, dusty, alkali plains west of the North Platte crossing. The water was, in fact, sweet and the river's swift, steady flow was perfect for bathing and washing clothes. The Sweetwater, however, had many twists and turns and the emigrants did not have the time to follow each major bend in the river overland. Their only alternative was to cross the river whenever it saved some time. The runoff from melting snow was not unusually heavy, water levels were not high, and the crossing decisions were easy ones as scores of earlier travelers had marked the best crossing points. Since no ferries or bridges were operating at this time the train would have to ford the Sweetwater nine times before reaching its end. The crossings were not particularly difficult, but the river was a hundred yards wide or more at many of the crossing points, the banks were littered with driftwood, and some crossings took as much as an entire day. Although the crossings resulted in a few minor injuries, no one on the train was killed or even seriously injured crossing the Sweetwater. Captain Billy was relieved that luck was on his side and remarked to Doc Brookings after the ninth and final crossing, "I hope you enjoyed your vacation. Things will get tougher from here on."

Fording the Sweetwater River

Ryan Walsh took advantage of both the close proximity of the train's campsites to the river and the longest days of the year to fish with Angus almost every evening during the two weeks that the train criss-crossed the Sweetwater. Ryan was pleasantly surprised as well that the character of his catch had changed from that he had caught on the North Platte. Trout were more plentiful and suckers less common making the evening fish fry that much more enjoyable. After her initial burst of enthusiasm, Neva was now an on and off participant in the fishing expeditions. She was often replaced, however, by Missy and Halo who, along with Angus, turned the outings into minor adventures. Missy proved to be a good worm catcher and Halo was a worthy challenger to Angus in the chase for hooked fish. John and Emma Marshall, the direct beneficiaries of Ryan's efforts, went along occasionally just to see if Missy was in safe hands and always found that she was.

Moving west along the Sweetwater, the train passed through the northern and western regions of The Red Desert, a high altitude desert comprised of sand dunes, rocky bluffs, and alkali flats. This area receives almost no rain and the little water it holds comes primarily from melting snow. Sagebrush and a few shrubs represent the only vegetation found there. Within the Red Desert lies the Great Divide Basin, a unique drainage basin where no water of any kind drains into an ocean. Even the waters of the Sweetwater, a part of the Mississippi River system, eventually reach the Gulf of Mexico. The basin did, however, provide a relatively low and easy passage across the Continental Divide, the point at which all water to the west drains to the Pacific Ocean and all water to the east drains into the Gulf of Mexico or Atlantic Ocean.

As the train approached the Continental Divide, the terrain became increasingly rugged and uphill. The strain on the animal teams was now showing and some of the wagons were having real problems keeping up even though Captain Billy had slowed the pace significantly once the train's climb into the foothills of the Rocky Mountains began. The emigrants now saw snow covered mountain peaks to the west for the first time.

The Trek across the Great Divide

(1869 painting by Albert Bierstadt)

On the last day of travel before reaching South Pass, two wagons overturned on steep, rocky sections of the trail as reminders to all that greater caution would be needed to cross the mountains ahead safely. Fortunately, no one was hurt in the mishaps although one oxen broke a leg and had to be shot. The overturned wagons blocked a narrow stretch of trail and had to be unloaded, made upright, and reloaded, stalling the train for several hours. Captain Billy announced that the delay would double as the midday break. The dead oxen was butchered during the break and provided a sumptuous dinner for all, including the dogs, later that evening.

The train arrived at South Pass on Day 65 and made camp for the night to prepare for the final ascent to the top. It was late June and the train was still slightly ahead of schedule. As a general rule, reaching South Pass before July 4th was necessary to beat the early snows that often fell in the mountains farther west. This relatively gentle break in the Rockies was discovered and made passable only six years earlier. The night before reaching South Pass Captain Billy met with his officers and together they made one of the most important decisions of the entire trip and that was to take what was known as the Sublette Cutoff across the arid wasteland due west of South Pass rather than travel along the original trail southwest to Fort Bridger and then turn back to the northwest to Fort Hall in what is now the southwest corner of Idaho. The cutoff would save the train forty six miles and three days of travel.

Their decision was based on the condition of the animal teams and livestock, the weather, the need for supplies, and so on, but it was a popular choice under most conditions for trains traveling to Oregon City. It was agreed that the cutoff represented no unacceptable risks, although it would be a hot and uncomfortable three or four days without water until the train reached the Green River. It would be particularly hard on the animal teams and cattle as they would have to go without food or water for all of that time. Captain Billy stressed the fact that water would be scarce in the days ahead and advised everyone to carry as much as possible when the train camped for the last time on the banks of the Sweetwater. After so many crossings leaving the Sweetwater River behind seemed like a good thing to some, but most did not appreciate how nice a drink of sweet water would be over the long, dry stretch ahead.

Traveling up and over South Pass presented a number of new challenges for the emigrants. Working against gravity, the climb to the top at an elevation of 6900 feet above sea level was arduous, but the descent was even worse as the risk of losing control of a wagon on the steep downhill sections of the trail was ever present. Wagons had to be unloaded and reloaded, pulleys and ropes were needed to hold the wagons back, and animal teams had to be unhitched and hitched to keep them from being restrained or struck by the stop and go movement of the wagons. Fortunately, the weather was good and Billy's train was able to negotiate the pass without suffering a major disaster.

From the summit of the pass, the travelers could see yet another geological landmark in the distance. Called The Table Rocks by earlier pioneers, these two flat-topped formations became known as The Oregon Buttes by the time Billy's train approached them. They were significant because they marked the eastern boundary of all land acquired by the United States from Great Britain in a treaty signed just a few years earlier. At the time, these western lands were called The Oregon Territory although they encompassed some or all of the present day states of Wyoming, Idaho, and Oregon. It was only midafternoon when the train arrived at the buttes, but Billy brought it to a halt for the day. He thought the emigrants could use the extra rest after struggling through the South

Pass descent and before the difficult trek across the Sublette Cutoff began. It would also be the last time the train had access to water for several days.

Just about everyone was already asleep when Billy and the cowboys allowed their campfire to burn out and drifted off as well. It was Jesse's turn to take the first watch that night. He sat down with his back against a large, flat rock to watch over the cattle grazing peacefully on the last grass they would see for days. It would be four long hours before another of the cowboys would relieve him.

A few hours into his shift Jesse heard the nearby neighing of a horse and wondered if one of theirs had escaped its nighttime corral. There was enough moonlight to see for some distance, but he saw or heard nothing unusual and again took his seat. Before he could get comfortable, Jesse heard something a second time, a noise he couldn't identify, and decided to walk around a bit to investigate, but as he stood up three men rushed at him from behind the rock against which he was resting and pressed the barrel of a gun to the side of his head. "Don't move, boy, or you're dead", one of the men whispered in Jesse's ear. They quickly tied Jesse's hands and feet, shoved a gag in his mouth, and knocked him to the ground. The leader of the three instructed one of the others, "Stay here and make sure he doesn't cause us any trouble. I'll bring your horse around." The three had a plan to rustle a manageable part of the herd and take them south along the Mormon Trail, only a short distance west of the buttes. They knew that with a good head start members of Billy's train would be unable to follow them too far in the wrong direction, especially when it would involve a round trip across a punishing desert.

69

The rustlers were headed for California by way of the Mormon and California Trails to mine for gold. Short of money, they hatched a plan to steal cattle to get them there. One would be eaten along the way and the rest sold on the black market in Fort Bridger, a trading post four days travel south on the Mormon trail or, perhaps later, when the rustlers reached Salt Lake City.

Dewdrop was a light sleeper and heard some of the cattle snorting and grunting as the rustlers attempted to separate them from the herd and move them toward the trail. Unlike the mooing of a contented animal, these were sounds of agitation and Dewdrop knew the difference. She slowly stood up and moved toward the cattle to see what the cause of the disturbance was. Upon reaching the herd, she knew immediately that something was wrong and began barking as loudly as she could. Her barking further riled up the cattle and they got noisier as well.

Rambles was the first to respond. He ran off to see what Dewdrop was up to, but found Jesse laying on the ground murmuring for help before reaching her. Rambles stood over Jesse barking until a light sleeping cowboy showed up to free him. It was only another minute or two before the commotion woke Captain Billy and the other cowboys and Jesse had reported the theft in progress. Unfortunately, there was little they could do quickly on foot. "Saddle up boys. We're being robbed!" Billy shouted.

It took several minutes for the cowboys to put on their boots, strap on their guns, reach their horses, and get them ready to ride. The rustlers had made off with about twenty head and were well down the trail before the cowboys were ready to give chase. Dewdrop, however, was running among the stolen cattle, barking up a storm, and doing her best to disrupt the rustlers' escape. That's when the first shots were fired. Recognizing that their plan to quietly make off with the cattle without being noticed had failed, one of the frustrated rustlers began shooting at Dewdrop in an effort to shut her up. Luckily, she was a small, fast moving target running among cows at night.

It didn't take long for Captain Billy and the cowboys to overcome the rustlers' short head start. Rambles had waited until Billy was on the move to join the chase and was now running hard to keep up with the men galloping on horseback. In an effort to avoid an all out gun battle Billy fired a warning shot into the air as he drew close to the fleeing cluster of men and cattle and shouted at them to stop. In the back of Billy's mind was the thought of what might happen to the train if he were no longer around to lead it. The rustlers, however, were not about to surrender and face the consequences of their act without a fight and began firing back over their shoulders at their pursuers. Realizing that the chase was not going to end peacefully, Billy gave the order to open fire, hoping still that no one would be killed.

The chase continued until the cattle had dispersed and were no longer a part of it and the rustlers saw that they could not outrun Billy and his boys. They decided to make their stand behind a large outcropping of rocks a few hundred feet from the trail. Once everyone had dismounted and taken cover the gunfire from both sides intensified. Crackling in the still of the night, the shots could be heard clearly by the emigrants lying in their tents several miles away. They now wondered what was going on and if they were in any danger.

A minute or two into the standoff Billy instructed the others, "Hold your fire boys. We've got 'em cornered and they'll be out of bullets soon." Rambles, of course, had his own ideas and continued to close in on the rustlers' position. In the shadowy darkness the excited rustlers began firing wildly at Rambles, mistaking his movement for someone sneaking up on them and wasting valuable ammo in the process. Rambles approach was low and erratic, a target only a marksman was likely to hit. By the time the rustlers saw it was only a large dog advancing toward them they were, in fact, almost out of ammo. It was time for them to give up and they did, but only two emerged from behind the rocks. The third was dead, killed by a lucky shot in the initial exchange of gunfire. With teeth bared, Rambles stood growling only a few feet from the two until the cowboys cautiously made their way to the surrender scene and took control.

Another hour went by before the horses and stolen cattle were rounded up and everyone made it back to camp. One of the cowboys had been shot in the arm, but the bullet passed cleanly through flesh only, and so Doc Brookings' repair job was a fairly simple one. "Keep that arm in a sling and don't use it for a while. I don't want to have to stitch it up over and over again," Brookings joked. Billy asked Jesse to explain what had happened to those on the train who were awake and asking questions and then interrogated the two surviving rustlers, recording their names and their stories and the details of their crime. He informed the prisoners that they would be taken to Fort Bridger by the emigrants leaving the train the next day to follow the Mormon Trail and handed over to the authorities there.

Billy also warned the two not to make any trouble along the way and reminded them that other remedies were still on the table with the words, "You're lucky we don't hang you right here." It was a long night for Billy and his boys. Billy's last thoughts before catching a few hours of sleep was the part Dewdrop and Rambles played in the drama and, looking for a bright side, the fact that the train had acquired three additional horses and some nice guns as a result of the attempted theft. The dead rustler was quickly and unceremoniously buried early the next morning in an unmarked grave.

CHAPTER 6 - PRAIRE DOGS AND BUFFALO

The train was late leaving the Oregon Buttes campsite the morning after its run in with the rustlers. It reached the Big Sandy River shortly after noon where Captain Billy ordered the midday break. It was here that the emigrants had their last chance to fill every available container to the brim with water, hopefully carrying enough to provide the horses and wagon teams with a few small drinks during the trip across The Green River Desert (later renamed The Little Colorado Desert). The cattle would have to go without. Only a short distance farther along the trail the train came to what was known as "The Parting of the Ways", the junction of the Oregon and Mormon Trails and the Sublette Cutoff. Where the trail split into two branches, dozens of messages of a general nature written by those who had already passed to be read by those who followed could be found attached to stakes driven into the hard, sun-baked ground.

The fifteen or so wagons that would be leaving the train at this point moved forward to receive some final instructions from Billy. He turned the rustlers and his written report of their attempted theft over to the leader of the smaller train, directing him to hand both over to the military authorities at Fort Bridger. He told the man in charge in a voice loud enough for the prisoners to hear, "If they act up, shoot 'em and dump their bodies at Bridger."

The Parting of the Ways

For the next three days the train traveled due west across the desert. The trail was hard and flat allowing several wagons to travel side by side thereby avoiding some of the dust that would have been raised by wagons ahead, but the heat was oppressive and there was no food or water for the animals. To avoid traveling during the hottest part of the day Billy got the train moving well before dawn each morning and ordered the midday break later than usual and for a longer time. Until the sun provided enough light to safely navigate the trail, some of the younger boys walked ahead of the train with lanterns to lead the way.

On the second day, the carcasses of dead cattle and oxen along the trail became commonplace. This made travel in the darkness even more difficult as man and beast alike were stumbling over the dead and, in some cases, dying livestock that lay on the trail. These were the animals unable to go on due to exhaustion, malnutrition, dehydration, or worn out hooves that were left behind by earlier trains. The sight and smell of the dead and dying animals only added to the emigrant's misery.

The cattle and animal teams traveling with Billy's train were in better condition than most, but on the third day the weakest of the stock gave out. Three head of cattle and three oxen were lost to the desert. Fortunately, the rustlers' horses were around to help pull a wagon that had lost half of its four oxen team. Permanent replacements for the fallen animals would be not be available until the train reached Fort Hall several weeks further along the trail. To the relief of all, the train finally reached the lush banks of the Green River early on the fourth day.

Captain Billy chose a campsite close to the river where grass for the livestock was plentiful, wood and water were nearby, and the train was close to the two ferries in operation at the time. Both ferry services, the Green River Mormon Ferry and the Robinson Ferry, were owned and operated by the Mormons at the time. The crossing of the Green River was one of the most treacherous the emigrants would encounter and the river had a long history of lost possessions, wagons, and lives in water not nearly as high as it was when Billy's train arrived.

Although the cost of crossing by ferry was high, the risks associated with fording the river were unacceptable and so there was no real alternative. Building rafts at the Green was not an option as the timber needed to do so was not available. It was often the case at this time of year that the encampments close to the ferries were full and the wait to cross the river several days long. Billy was lucky his train arrived after two others had just crossed, a prime campsite was available, and the ferries were available the very next day. Since each ferry could handle about forty wagons a day, Billy decided to use both services and cross the sixty wagons that remained in his train on the same day. After the exhausting trip across the desert and a laborious river crossing, Billy decided that the following day would be a day of rest and recovery. The cowboys and the cattle would spend the day that the wagons were crossing regaining some strength and then swim the river the following day at a wider, shallower, slower moving point a short distance downstream.

Shortly after the train made camp on the near side of the river, the emigrants enjoyed a big dinner of roasted beef courtesy of the fallen cattle. The cattle, animal teams, and horses ate and drank at the bank of the river until their bloated bellies hung low. Captain Billy was busy negotiating with the ferry operators, dividing the wagons into the two ferry groups, and notifying the wagon owners where to report the next morning.

Dewdrop and Rambles visited the Marshall and Walsh wagons for the first time since the march across the desert began as the long days in the hot sun left them in no mood for socializing in the evening. Missy Marshall was delighted to have her group of four back together. Dewdrop and Rambles, though still a little wobbly, did their best to be sociable. Ryan Walsh eyed the river wondering what might be lurking beneath the surface, but didn't have the energy to fish that day. Ryan and John Marshall traded stories of ferry disasters they had heard about, but dismissed them as the products of poorly trained or drunken operators. "I don't think we'll have any problems with the operators here," John remarked, "After all, they're Mormons." Practically everyone found an excuse to turn in early that evening and by the time it was dark the camp was quiet.

The next morning the emigrants hitched up their teams according to their scheduled crossing time and moved their wagons into position at the site of their assigned ferry. Captain Billy was in the middle of it all directing traffic and trying to keep things organized. Dewdrop and the cowboys were moving the herd downstream to their crossing point, allowing the cattle to leisurely graze their way along the river bank. Once the herd was out of sight of the others, Jesse shouted, "It's bath time, boys. I can't stand your stink any longer!" Enthusiastically stripping off all of their clothes, they jumped one by one off the river bank into a deep, swirling eddy near the shoreline. Although Dewdrop had never made such a leap, she hesitated only momentarily before belly flopping into the water with the others. She quickly found that her legs were too short to reach the bottom in the waist deep water where the cowboys were splashing around and, after a short swim among them, retreated to wallow in shallower water close to shore. After half an hour of spirited horseplay, Dewdrop and the boys had had enough and climbed out of the water clean and refreshed. Jesse reminded the boys that their clothes needed washing as well and, although they agreed, they made short work of it.

By late afternoon almost all of the wagons and animal teams had been ferried across and the train had established a campsite on the western side of the river. It was then that Billy saw another train pulling into the encampment area his train had just left and the arrival of a scout from a second train not far behind. Although it was luck, his timing could not have been better. By the time the last of Billy's wagons arrived at the campsite, those that had crossed earlier were already eating their dinners.

There was no rush that night since the train would have the following day to get ready for the next leg of the journey. There was, however, an urgent call for Doc Brookings early in the evening. A pregnant woman was about to give birth and the expectant father wanted Brookings to oversee the event. Captain Billy was not in favor of births on the trail, but the timing of these things was not within his control. "Doc, is there anything I can do?" Billy asked.

"I hope not," Doc replied. It was well after midnight before the cry of a newborn baby broke the nighttime silence. "It's a girl!" Doc proclaimed, "And she looks to be a healthy one at that. Do you have a name for her?"

The new mother and father looked at each other for an answer before the father said "No, not yet, but we'll have plenty of time to think about it on the trail."

"OK, when you decide on one, let me know and I'll make out a birth certificate," Doc replied. Once everything seemed to be under control Brookings left the couple and their child thinking to himself how difficult life on the trail might be for a newborn.

The emigrants awoke in the morning feeling much better than they did the day before. They would have time that day to make repairs, write letters, take baths, wash clothes, and generally take it easy before the train hit the trail again the next day. Jesse and Dewdrop, on the other hand, would be working with the cowboys to get the herd across the river. The cattle crossing went pretty much as planned. The access and exit points were not steep, the bottom was firm, the current was not swift, and the crossing site included some shallower areas where the cattle could walk rather than swim. Dewdrop, however, would have to swim the entire width of the river and once she entered the water she paddled hard without stopping until she reached the other side only a hundred feet or so downstream of where she started. No cattle were lost and the crossing took only half a day so the cowboys got some additional rest as well.

Ryan and Neva Walsh took advantage of the break by doing a little fishing, but for the first time since the trip began his line remained limp wherever he threw it. A frustrated Angus sat upright studying the water, but there was no reward for his patience. "Maybe it's the wrong time of day or maybe there's a hatch of flies the fish are eating," Ryan theorized.

Whatever the reason, a disappointed Neva remarked, "I guess it's bacon and beans for dinner again."

Just as Ryan was about to quit, his line tightened and began moving upstream. "Wait a minute. I think I've got something!" he whispered to Neva. After a short pause he set the hook, realized that he had something big on the line, and hoisted a large, writhing, snake-like creature out of the water and onto the riverbank.

"Eek!" cried Neva, "It's an eel!" Angus was on it like a shot, but the slimy, rapidly twisting thing easily eluded his grip. Ryan quickly intervened to end a potentially messy tangle between dog and eel. "You're not going to keep that thing, are you?" Neva asked.

"Of course. They're good eating and besides I'll need to kill it to get my hook back," Ryan replied.

"Well, I hope you and Angus enjoy it. It's still bacon and beans for me," she said.

Knowing well that the eel would look far more appetizing once it was skinned and roasted, Ryan's reply was simply, "We'll see."

The train had traveled only a few hundred yards the next morning before passing a large, brownish, sandstone cliff known as Names Hill. Located only a few steps from the trail, Names Hill was the third of the three places travelers stopped to carve their names. Carvings dated as early as 1827 could be found on the face of the bluff and, over time, the number of inscriptions on the rock eventually reached two thousand. Of interest to most were the undated Indian carvings that were made long before the westward migration of white men began. Those interested in making their mark on the cliff did so the day before as the cliff was only a short walk from the Green River campsite and Captain Billy made it clear that that the train would not be stopping at the rock once it was underway the next day.

The trail west of the Green River became progressively rougher and more mountainous, crossing first over Oyster Ridge and then veering southwest across the Pomeroy Basin to the southern end of Commissary Ridge. Travelling around rather than over the ridge was the only practical option. The train had just stopped for the day on the south side of Commissary Ridge when the emigrants saw a herd of buffalo in the basin below approaching from the south. It was their first sighting of buffalo since the trip began. As they watched the herd moving closer, it looked like a streaming swarm of black dots that stretched for miles with no apparent end. Some of the men traveling on horseback were anxious to begin a hunt when Captain Billy intervened. He told them, "It'll be dark soon and I don't want you shooting or messing with your kill at night. They'll still be around in the morning." It was good advice, but meant a restless night for those who intended to hunt the next day.

What the emigrants saw were not actually buffalo, but North American bison, a very different animal. The true buffalo lives only in Asia and does not have the huge head, thick beard, or large shoulder hump that characterize the bison. Bison also have much shorter and sharper horns than do buffalo. They don't see well, but have excellent senses of hearing and smell. It has been estimated that as many as sixty million bison roamed the American plains before they were hunted for their hides and indiscriminately slaughtered into virtual extinction by traders and settlers. Their gradual disappearance was an important reason the indigenous Indian populations fell at the same time. There were perhaps twenty five million remaining when Billy's train traveled the trail, but by 1860, only ten years later, their numbers had been reduced to a scant one thousand.

Early the next morning Jesse and six others were eagerly preparing for the hunt, cleaning and loading their rifles, saddling their horses, and planning their strategy. The buffalo had paused for the night, but the herd now stretched as far as the eye could see to both the north and the south. They were apparently following a river just west of the camp known as Ham's Fork.

Although the campsite was located on higher ground and seemed to be out of the herd's path, Captain Billy reminded the hunters that once the shooting started, the agitated animals would probably stampede. The last thing he wanted was fifty thousand buffalo trampling through the campsite, stories of which were legend on the trail. Billy further cautioned them, "Remember, these animals can weigh a ton, run almost forty miles an hour, jump almost six feet straight up, and have very bad tempers."

As the hunters digested Billy's words, Jesse added, "We shouldn't kill more than a few. We'd need too much time and too many oxen to haul more than that back to camp, so we'll butcher a couple where they lie and bring back only the good parts." Dewdrop and Rambles were sitting side by side patiently watching the preparations, waiting to join the hunt once it began.

"Good luck and take your time," Billy shouted as the hunters and the dogs took off toward the migrating herd. Billy knew the train couldn't move on until the herd had cleared the trail and that was likely to take at least the rest of the day, if not longer.

Halo and Angus were also up and about, wandering around their wagons waiting for breakfast to be served when they saw and heard something interesting in the distance. Dozens of chubby little critters were scurrying from one hole in the ground to another, standing upright in groups, and chattering among themselves. Both Halo and Angus were bred to hunt rats and other underground dwellers and, after studying the curious creatures for a minute or two, succumbed to their instincts and ran off on their own hunt. Missy noticed the dogs heading toward the floor of the basin and asked her mother, "Can I use our spyglass to keep an eye on the dogs?"

"Of course, dear," Emma replied. Producing a small telescope from the Marshall wagon, she and Missy took turns following the movements of the dogs and, much farther away, the buffalo hunt. It was quite a show.

Once the buffalo were within range, the hunters slowed their approach to get as close as possible to the herd before spooking the animals. The rifles Jesse and the others carried were single shot muzzle loaders which required the gunpowder and then the bullet to be dropped down the barrel and rammed into place before a shot could be fired. It was therefore important to make every shot count as reloading alongside the moving herd would be an awkward operation at best. On Jesse's signal each hunter was to ride with the herd along its edge, pick out a target, take his best shot at close range, and then move away from the herd to meet with the others and assess the results.

The Buffalo Hunt

(Original sketch in Oregon Trail Museum)

Rambles and Dewdrop played no practical part in the hunt, but were not to be denied a bit of excitement and ran among the buffalo for the sheer fun of it. After the first shot was fired, however, the buffalo close by panicked and went from an uneasy trot to a full run and, once the stampede began, the two dogs found that exiting the herd would not be as easy as it was to enter. There was just no opening in the stream of fast moving animals through which an escape to the outside of the herd was possible. The two were running as fast as they could just to stay ahead of the animals bearing down on them from behind and realized that a decision of some kind would have to be made before they ran out of gas. Rambles made the first move and it was toward the inside of the herd. Dewdrop followed his lead and the two gradually weaved their way from the stampeding animals on the edge of the herd to slower moving animals farther from the gunshots. Working their way against the flow through parts of the herd unaffected by the hunt, they safely made a wide circle back to their starting point. Though successful, the maneuver took almost an hour to complete.

The hunters firing first found the buffalo to be easy targets, but those firing last had to shoot at fast moving targets while at a full gallop. When the dust cleared, three buffalo lay dead. A few others were probably wounded, but not fatally, and were still running with the herd. It would have been possible from the location of the dead animals and the order in which the hunters fired to figure out who killed what, but Jesse did his best to confuse the issue so that everyone could claim that it was his shot that brought down one of the huge beasts. He asked one of the hunters to have a wagon with room to spare brought out to the site to carry the meat and hides back to camp and said to the others, "OK, let's dress these things out. There'll be more than enough for everyone."

The hunters were working on the third carcass when Rambles and Dewdrop finally completed their return trip. Jesse saw that Dewdrop was limping badly and, laying aside his knife, took a break to examine her leg. "What happed old girl? Get stepped on by a buffalo?" he asked.

If Dewdrop could have answered, her answer would have been, "It's no joke. I was nearly killed!" She licked her bloody foot and Jesse's bloody hands and then flopped to the ground staring in anticipation at the pile of buffalo remains that would soon be hers.

While the buffalo hunt was going on, Angus and Halo were in pursuit of white-tailed prairie dogs, a species once so common that hundreds of millions of them populated the upper Midwest and western states. These relatives of the squirrel live in family groups in underground colonies called "towns" and are known for their extensive vocabulary, perhaps the most advanced of any animal language ever decoded. Their barks and squeaks have extremely detailed meanings and can convey to others, among other things, the specific type of threat confronting them. The sound of their call led many settlers to refer to them as "sod poodles". They are food for just about every predator that lives in their range, including hawks, owls, snakes, coyotes, wolves, badgers, and ferrets. Nonetheless, prairie dogs are skilled fighters with sharp claws and powerful teeth and are capable of fighting back with a fury. Over short distances they can race along at speeds of thirty five miles an hour. Due to loss of habitat over time and their susceptibility to bubonic plague, a disease spread by infected fleas, the number of white-tailed prairie dogs today is only a tiny fraction of what it once was.

Missy and Emma sat side by side on a large rock watching Halo and Angus working as a team in their effort to catch one of the many prairie dogs popping up and then disappearing all around them. As it turned out, killing a buffalo was much easier than catching the fast and elusive prairie dogs. One of the canines would chase the rodents down a hole while the other crouched at a nearby exit waiting for something to emerge. Nothing ever did. Angus was the more aggressive of the two and made numerous attempts to follow his prey into its burrow, disappearing for minutes at a time before reappearing with nothing to show for his effort. Halo had not forgotten the trouble she got into the last time she took off on a varmint hunt and looked back toward the encampment occasionally to make sure it was still in sight.

There were so many holes so close to camp that one of the girls always had a good view of the action through the spyglass. John Marshall and a few others joined the audience once the sound of rifle shots were heard. John commandeered the spyglass for a moment to view the buffalo hunt, but it was pretty much over once the shots were fired. He could only distinguish the hunters from the hunted, but confidently remarked, "I think there'll be fresh meat on the fire tonight." Interest in the dog show was not universal and everyone but Missy and Emma quickly drifted away once Emma described what she had seen of the buffalo hunt.

Having worn themselves out playing their version of Whack-A-Mole, Angus and Halo were about to give it up when an eagle, apparently watching the proceedings from high above, swooped down with talons extended and tried to grab Halo. Fortunately, it was a miss, but this unexpected turn of events ended the hunt abruptly and the dogs beat a hasty retreat back to the safety of the camp. Angus reported in a bloody mess. What went on out of sight must have been quite a fight and Missy wondered if Angus had given as good as he got. Missy and Halo walked

Angus back to the Walsh wagon to explain his wounds to Neva. After determining that Angus' condition was not serious, Neva just shook her head and said to him, "I was wondering what you were up to. I hope you had fun."

The trail was clear of buffalo shortly before noon and Billy decided that it was worth moving on even though the day on the trail would be a short one. The train forded Ham's Fork only a mile from camp and crossed over the Ham's Fork Plateau during the afternoon hours. The train camped that night at a location on the east side of Dempsey Ridge called Emigrant Springs, a popular stopover site named for the spring that feeds Emigrant Creek. That evening everyone on the train enjoyed a dinner of roasted buffalo steaks and washed it down with sweet spring water. Billy estimated that the hunters had brought back about seven hundred pounds of meat. Any that was not consumed at dinner was dried over campfires to be eaten later. The dogs all got their share. Rambles and Dewdrop would have eaten more if it were not for the fact that they gorged themselves on the meaty bones and organs of that third carcass earlier in the day. It was a long, lethargic afternoon for both, but it beat traveling on an empty stomach.

A few hours after the train broke camp, it began the difficult climb to the summit of Dempsey Ridge. Once again, unneeded items were discarded to ease the strain on the weaker, smaller animal teams. The descent was much steeper and far more dangerous than the ascent. It went slowly, but there were no serious wagon accidents. It was almost dark before the train left Dempsey Ridge behind and Captain Billy located a suitable campsite. Billy pushed the train farther that day than he ordinarily would have for a reason. He declared the following day, Thursday July 4th, a travel holiday. The emigrants and their stock could again rest up and celebrate the birth of the nation. There would be time for the women to prepare a holiday meal and wash clothes in a nearby creek, the men to make repairs and do a little drinking, the children to play some games, and the dogs to roam around under foot looking for handouts. It was well after dark by the time the emigrants made camp. Most had a cold supper and went directly to bed.

In the morning the campers discovered that there was no wood to burn anywhere around the campsite. As the traffic on all of the trails increased, many of the things that nature provided, including firewood, became scarce. The plateaus and basins between the ridges, however, were buffalo migration routes and the material they left behind was often used as a source of fuel, producing an even, odorless flame. Fortunately, the train was camped in such a place. The task of collecting the hardened dung was not a pleasant one and so a contest for the children was devised by one of the more inventive emigrants. Each participant was given a sack and those filling the most sacks by mid-morning would win a prize. The children were reminded, however, that anyone with anything soft in their sack would be disqualified! Curious, Billy asked the event organizer what the prizes were. "I have no idea," the man answered. "What do you have in those supply wagons that would be of interest to children?" The contest turned out to be more fun than it should have been. The children discovered that many of the droppings were hard, flat discs that could be thrown like Frisbees and so they created their own games within the dung collection game. They threw the discs to each other and to Dewdrop and Rambles who quickly learned to catch them on the fly. Sitting around their campfires enjoying the day off, the emigrants joked about the "firepoop" in countless ways. The boredom of the journey was showing on young and old alike.

CHAPTER 7 - SHOSHONE COUNTRY

The day after the holiday respite, the train came to the intersection of the western end of the Sublette Cutoff and the main trail coming from Fort Bridger to the south. Traffic on the trail would be heavier and campsites more difficult to find from this point on as travelers from both routes were again on the same path. Traveling along the north shore of the Bear River, the train reached Thomas Fork, a tributary of the Bear, the next day. Thomas Fork was not particularly deep or swift, but it was notorious for its steep, muddy banks. Getting down into and then out of the stream were so difficult that two bridges were built across it just a few years later.

The following day the train would be confronted with the arduous ascent and dangerous descent over a ridge known as The Big Hill. The Big Hill was the only way around an impassable cut the Bear River made through the mountains. Captain Billy chose a campsite close to the base of The Big Hill just in case a full day was needed to get the entire train up and over the ridge. Another train was not far behind and, since it would have to make camp nearby, Billy informed everyone that the train would be hitting the trail early to avoid any delays that might result from following another train up and over the ridge. Knowing that it would cheer some of the emigrants while depressing others, he also announced that the train had now travelled about one thousand miles, roughly half the distance to its destination.

Although the emigrants had a chance to study The Big Hill from afar from their campsite, most underestimated the toll the long climb would take on their animal teams. More than a few wagons needed help making the climb by "borrowing" oxen from others and adding them to their own teams. More difficult still was holding the wagons back and under control on the way down. It was late afternoon by the time Dewdrop and the cowboys moved the last of the cattle to the bottom of the ridge and the train made camp for the night. The Big Hill was an exhausting experience for all, but everyone and everything made it over without a serious mishap.

The dogs were among the few with the energy to do anything but eat and sleep after negotiating The Big Hill. Halo and Angus, after all, crossed the ridge in the relative comfort of their wagons and Dewdrop and Rambles covered far less ground on their feet than they would have on a typical day. Missy and her group of four met for their evening ritual as usual, but John and Emma ended the affair early so that they and their immediate neighbors could get a little extra sleep. The dogs did not seem all that disappointed.

Descending the Big Hill

(1849 sketch by pioneer James F. Wilkins)

The train followed the Bear River through the Bear River Valley for the next eighty miles. This proved to be a very pleasant four day trip along the trail. The scenery was spectacular, the river was clean and blue, good grasses and timber were abundant, and fishing and hunting opportunities were plentiful. After weeks of travel through deserts and over mountains the change was a welcome relief that raised the spirits of those that needed it most.

Captain Billy was looking forward to stopping the train for its midday break near Peg Leg Smith's, a trading post opened just two years earlier by a one-legged mountain man named Thomas Smith. Smith was quite the businessman, providing supplies, horses, and cattle at high prices to those headed to California to search for gold. Billy had met Smith soon after the post opened in 1848 on his last trip along the trail, but found the four cabins and the Indian lodges that comprised the post abandoned when he arrived. Rambles sniffed around the vacant post for several minutes before trotting back to Billy without a sign of life to report. "Rambles old boy, I guess Peg Leg made his money fast and left to work that gold mine he always bragged he'd found," Billy murmured.

The train reached Clover Creek, the site of the next planned stopover, late that afternoon only to find the prime campsite already occupied. Billy's scout had staked out a suitable area a bit farther from the water, but still readily accessible to it, and the train made camp there for the night. Billy asked his officers to spread the word that they were now deep into Shoshone Indian country and, although an organized attack on the train was not a threat, solo attempts to steal livestock or supplies were a possibility. The night watchmen were instructed to be extra vigilant from this point in the journey on.

It was two days later that Captain Billy, riding a hundred yards or so ahead of the train, saw several small groups of elk drinking at the river's edge. Once commonplace, sightings of deer, elk, and antelope along the trail had become increasingly rare due to the hunting pressure associated with the almost continuous flow of wagons. Some of the animals were killed, but most were simply driven to more secure locations. Billy thought an elk and bird hunt would be much appreciated by the hunters among the emigrants, himself included, and called the train to a halt early in the afternoon to allow them this opportunity.

The elk hunters included Captain Billy, Jesse, two of the emigrants traveling on horseback, and, of course, Rambles. Billy wanted to restrict the size of his group to a few experienced hunters that had some chance of bagging an elk. The bird hunting party, on the other hand, was comprised of John Marshall, two of the cowboys, and more than a dozen others. A few possessed a firearm and ammunition appropriate for shooting birds, but most did not. This group would hunt on foot working their way along the river's edge. Billy instructed the cowboys, neither of which would be an active shooter, to go along primarily to supervise the hunt as several of the participants had little hunting experience, would be shooting with inappropriate weapons, and were involved just to relieve their boredom. As the birdmen marched off in the direction of the river, Dewdrop decided at the last instant to tag along with them and her cowboy friends. Once the group was out of earshot, Billy confided to Jesse, "I hope they all come back alive."

Jesse thought for only an instant before replying, "I doubt it."

After a few minutes of strategic planning, Billy and the others rode off in the opposite direction. Their plan was to ride several miles downriver, locate elk trails and crossing points along the river bank, and then wait for the bird hunters to begin shooting. The shots, they reasoned, would spook the animals in their direction. Billy had no doubt the bird hunters would shoot at anything and everything and Rambles had no difficulty leading the hunters to the routes the elk traveled daily. After deciding on a likely area, Billy and the others split up, each taking up a different position to establish several shooting lanes. Before they parted,

Billy reminded the others, "Wait for a good shot. We'll probably get only one chance." Their vigil did not last long. Intermittent volleys of gunshots in the distance began almost immediately and, peeking out from their hiding places, the hunters waited anxiously for something to happen. Willing to let the others take their best shots first, Billy was focused on keeping Rambles hidden.

After some time had passed and tensions had eased a bit, Jesse was the first to notice movement not where it was expected, but on the other side of the river. There trotted three cows and a bull elk, moving away from the gunshots in the direction of the hunters. Jesse was the closest of the four to the river and, after hand signaling to the others that he was going to take a shot, he fired. As his shot echoed off the neighboring hillsides, the bull looked back across the river in Jesse's direction for a moment and then fell like a stone to the ground. The cows bolted off before any of the others could get a decent shot away. It may have been a lucky shot, but it was the only one the group would end up taking that day. After gathering to congratulate Jesse, the fact that his trophy lay on the other side of the river began to sink in. Billy stated the obvious, "We've got our work cut out for us now. Good thing the river is low."

Working quickly, the four of them managed to return to the campsite laden with fresh meat and daylight to spare. Their success came at a small price and that was their wet socks and underwear. Jesse rode in holding the elk's impressive rack of antlers high over his head, but tossed them aside as he dismounted. "No place to carry these," he lamented.

The bird hunters had returned much earlier, but were still discussing their adventure when Billy and his group made it back to camp. Apparently, they considered their hunt a success as well. They killed six ducks, two crows, three songbirds, and two jack rabbits. One of the cowboys in charge of the hunt reported to Billy, "It was chaos. The ducks and rabbits were all killed by John Marshall and one other, the only two with shotguns. Everything else was killed in wild hails of gunfire from the others." He added that if Dewdrop had not retrieved most of the ducks from the river they would still be floating somewhere downstream and that she spent so much time in the line of fire that it was a miracle she was not shot.

The job of cleaning the ducks and rabbits for the grill turned out to be a skill that few engaged in the hunt possessed and so it was left to John and Emma Marshall to dress the kill. The crows and the songbirds never saw the heat of the campfire and were discarded with the inedible portions of the ducks and rabbits. A community roast was enjoyed by all that night with Rambles and Dewdrop each getting a share for their part in the hunts. Billy had not forgotten to haul the elk's organs back as a special treat for the dogs. Angus and Halo were front and center as well, but were content with seconds off the plates of the Marshalls and the Walshes plus a few choice morsels Missy was able to sneak to them.

Two days later the train arrived at Soda Springs, a geologically active area the emigrants agreed was the most interesting sight they had seen yet. They witnessed dozens of springs of different colors spewing carbonated mineral water up from the ground through cone-shaped openings, some of them smelling of sulfur, some hot, some warm, and some cold. At a nearby location known as Steamboat Spring, the emigrants were fascinated by a small geyser of carbonated water that sounded much like the whistle of a steamboat when it erupted. The train arrived at Soda Springs early in the afternoon, but stopped for the day to allow everyone to enjoy the sights, take a bath or wash clothes in the bubbling hot springs, and, for those inclined to do so, record their observations in journals. Captain Billy warned the emigrants not to drink too much of the "soda" water as the high alkali content was known to make some sick.

As Halo and the Marshalls headed off to explore the springs, Angus announced to Neva with a bark that he was leaving the campsite to join them. Before the group was too far off Neva shouted to Missy, "Please keep an eye on Angus. We want him back in one piece!" The two dogs experienced the springs not from their edges, but from inside them, frolicking in the frothy waters, biting at the bubbles, and enjoying a hot bath for the first time ever.

Missy eventually turned to her mother and said, "I wish I was having as much fun as Halo."

"Go right in if you want to," Emma replied.

Missy removed only her socks and shoes before wading waist deep into the inviting pool where the dogs were playing and squatted down until the warm, effervescent water reached her shoulders. "This is nice," she cooed, "Why don't you come in?"

John and Emma were planning to bathe later in a more private setting, not fully clothed in the presence of other sightseers. John politely told Missy, "Maybe later."

Missy and the dogs were still soaking wet when they got back to camp and Angus jumped into Neva's arms. "Well, you smell better than you did when you left," Neva remarked. "Let's hope those bubbling waters kill fleas too."

Less than half a day's travel from Soda Springs the train passed Sheep Rock, the name given to a small, isolated mountain rising several hundred feet above the Bear River and populated by mountain sheep often sighted by earlier travelers. No sheep were seen, however, on the day Billy's train passed it. It was here as well that the river, which eventually emptied into the Great Salt Lake, made a sweeping U-turn to the southwest and the trail turned to the northwest. The pleasant journey along the Bear was over.

Just as Captain Billy was about to stop the train for its midday break, he came face to face with a group of six Shoshone Indians on horseback. Traveling with them were two large dogs, both of which looked to have more than a little wolf in their bloodline. Fortunately, one of the Shoshone spoke just enough English to communicate with Billy although the conversation was limited and hand gestures were needed to complete most of the exchanges. They were hunters from a nearby encampment traveling along the trail to reach a popular hunting site. Billy invited them to have lunch with him and the cowboys and, after an awkward pause and some discussion among the Indians, they accepted.

The Shoshone, a name meaning "high growing grasses" in the Shoshone language, was the dominant tribe in what is now southern Idaho and it was not unexpected that the emigrants would come into contact with them along this stretch of trail. There were very few violent clashes between Indians and emigrants in general before 1850 and most of the tribes were tolerant of, if not downright helpful to, the wagon trains passing through their territories. It was not unusual, however, for an emigrant to travel the entire length of the trail without ever seeing an Indian. In all, only 360 emigrants were killed by Indians between the years 1840 and 1860 while 426 Indians were killed by emigrants during the same period. More settlers were, in fact, killed by accidentally shooting themselves than were killed as a result of Indian attacks. Most of the Indian-related deaths took place west of South Pass, many of these occurring along the Snake River in Shoshone country in the years after Billy's train passed their way and peace between the Shoshone and the white man had ended.

Luncheon with the Shoshone was a cordial affair. Billy's contribution to the menu consisted of bacon, beans, and coffee while the Indians offered up a variety of dried meats, berries, and nuts. The cowboys couldn't identify the kind of meat the Indians carried from its taste, but decided it would be best to let it remain a mystery. Billy wondered if it was dog meat which he knew was a part of the Indian diet.

Rambles and Dewdrop sat side by side studying the Indian dogs who sat together on the opposite side of the lunch circle watching them. The staring contest ended when Rambles decided to drift around to their

101

side of the circle to find out if they were as tough as they looked. As he approached them from behind, they got to their feet, turned toward him, bared their teeth, and began to growl. Rambles then began to dart back and forth in a playful manner to see what kind of response this would produce. Everyone was now watching the dogs with interest, unsure if the interaction would end in a dog fight or not. It did not.

Recognizing Rambles' gesture as a friendly one, the Indian dogs' demeanor changed and, after a minute or two of tentative butt sniffing, they joined Rambles in a game of tag. Once the visiting dogs had passed Rambles' test, Dewdrop joined the group and the four dogs ran together in great circles in an effort to outdo each other. Billy tried to keep one eye on the pack, but the dogs disappeared from sight for several minutes more than once. Each time they did, one of the Shoshone would cup his hands to his mouth and make a loud call that brought them back almost immediately. Billy and the boys marveled at the obedience of the Indian dogs, probably only one step removed from wild wolves.

As the luncheon came to an end, Billy presented the Shoshone with a small bag of coffee as a parting gift after which they and the train continued on their separate ways. It would be another two days before the train reached Fort Hall and the Snake River.

The next day the train traveled through the "lava lands", a stark, desolate plain of lava flows sparsely covered with soil, and passed the waypoints known as The Three Buttes. Rising high above the surrounding plain, these buttes are solidified domes of lava pushed up through volcanic fissures in the earth a half million years ago. Progress along the hard, smooth trail was good and the train reached Fort Hall early the next afternoon. Built in 1834 as a fur trading post, Fort Hall became the most important resupply station in the Snake River Valley and a stopover site for every traveler that passed its way.

Before 1843 the trail west of Fort Hall was not well established and emigrants had to abandon their wagons at the fort and continue west on foot with their animals or on horseback. Because it was located at the western end of a long stretch of trail common to all of the trails to the far west, Fort Hall was always very crowded during the emigration season. When Billy's train arrived several others were already there. Luckily, a good campsite had been vacated earlier that day and Billy's train was able to move right into it. The ashes of the campfires were still glowing. Billy noticed immediately that it was the flag of United States flag flying over the fort rather than the British flag as it was when he was last there just a few years ago. He learned later that night that the United States had acquired a huge hunk of the west that included the fort from Britain only a year earlier and that The Hudson Bay Company, a British concern, relinquished operation of the fort at that time.

The stopover at Fort Hall gave the travelers a chance to purchase any needed food or supplies and to compare notes with emigrants from other trains. It was also the place to trade with the Shoshone who were camped just outside the fort during the emigration season for that purpose. The items the emigrants most often received in these trades were buffalo robes, moccasins, honey, and dried meats and fish. The list of things the Shoshone wanted in return was a long one. It included tobacco, knives, jewelry, mirrors, needles and thread, cloth, ribbons, and processed food items like flour, coffee and sugar. Although always of great interest to the Indians, Captain Billy forbid the trading of firearms and ammunition. Billy had stowed a number of these items in one of the supply wagons for just such an occasion and traded some rings and necklaces and a few mirrors for an ample supply of honey, a pure food that never goes bad that he knew he could trust. It would sweeten the cowboys' coffee and, hopefully, their dispositions as well.

Trading with the Shoshone at Fort Hall

John Marshall was among the traders and returned to his wagon with a gift for Emma, a stylish winter coat of buffalo hair that would come in handy a few months later in the year. He also traded for some smoked salmon, a staple of tribes living near rivers that flowed to the Pacific, but a treat none of the emigrants had experienced prior to their stop at Fort Hall. John was anxious to share it with Ryan and Neva Walsh at dinner as payback for the many fresh fish dinners Ryan had provided the Marshalls.

Ryan Walsh had little money and nothing to trade and so spent the daylight hours of the stopover exploring a section of the Snake River that ran near the fort. The Snake was a river of great importance in the region, stretching 1078 miles from its headwaters in what is now western Wyoming to the point where it emptied into the Columbia River in present day Washington State. The emigrants would see a lot of it from this point on. As he and Angus approached the river, Ryan noticed two Shoshone Indians fiddling with some kind of trap at the water's edge. He introduced himself with only a nod of his head and watched as they picked their catch from a loosely woven basket and placed it into a sack. He drew closer to see exactly what it was they were catching, but the answer came to him a second before seeing the creatures. They were trapping crayfish, those tasty little fresh water lobsters that he had overlooked since the trip began. He made a quick study of the trap before the Indians placed some chopped up entrails into it as bait and tossed it back into the water. Staked to the shoreline with short lengths of rope, the traps were emptied every few days.

Energized by the thought that he could set his own traps each evening and harvest them each morning to supplement his wagon's food supply, Ryan quickly returned to his wagon to begin work on the traps he had already designed in his head. He knew crayfish were also an excellent bait and figured the critters would improve his fishing in the bargain. It was obvious to Neva that Ryan was excited about something as he flitted here and there searching for construction materials. Neva finally asked, "What are you doing?"

"I saw something down at the river I have to try. There's a lobster dinner in it for you," Ryan replied. Neva wasn't quite sure what he meant but decided to wait until Ryan had calmed down before asking again.

The thing about Fort Hall most likely to stick in the memories of the emigrants were the mosquitoes. As day faded to dusk, swarms of them moved into the encampments surrounding the fort to feed, harassing the livestock and forcing everyone to devise some kind of cover up for protection. Captain Billy and the cowboys were slapping themselves silly throughout dinner and Dewdrop and Rambles, unable to relax, moved about constantly in an effort to keep the relentless insects from lighting on and biting them. "Don't the Indians have something for this?" Jesse asked.

Busy tying blankets around Bucket to afford him some relief Billy replied, "Don't know, but it's midsummer, there's lots of water nearby, and our stink is a surefire mosquito magnet." It was a long, uncomfortable night for those most susceptible to the pests.

CHAPTER 8 - THE THREE ISLAND CROSSING

After leaving Fort Hall, the train would travel on the south side of the Snake River for 180 miles. Along this entire leg of the journey, the river remained buried in a deep canyon and so the emigrants had little or no access to its waters. An alternate route north of the river was established by later travelers with the courage to ford the river at relatively slow moving points near Fort Hall, but many lost their wagons and animal teams in these difficult crossings and the northern route never became a popular one.

On the third day out of Fort Hall, the trail passed American Falls, the first of several impressive waterfalls on the Snake. Dropping almost two hundred feet from its top to the river below, the falls could be heard well before it was seen. As the train approached the falls, its rumble became a roar and the curious stopped briefly to take a look.

Late the next day, the train arrived at a distinctive cluster of large boulders that came to be known as The Devil's Gate, so named by the settlers because it represented an ideal point of attack for the Shoshone. In 1862 it was renamed Massacre Rocks after a deadly skirmish with the Indians occurred near the rocks. Because this was one of the few places where the river was accessible, it was a natural stopover site and Billy's train was no exception.

Ryan Walsh had passed the evenings since the train left Fort Hall working on his prototype crayfish trap. Using odds and ends borrowed from fellow travelers and things nature provided along the trail, he cobbled together a rather professional looking device that he believed was an improvement over the traps used by the Indians and was now anxious to give it a try. Since he and Neva were going down to the river to collect water anyway, this was as good a time as any. He would set the trap that evening and then run down to the river and retrieve it in the morning. His bait was a small hunk of rotting meat Ryan had cut from the carcass of a dead cow he saw lying on the side of the trail earlier that day. Angus was forced to share his wagon with the stinking stuff much of the afternoon and was happy to see it go. Needless to say, Neva thought a tainted wagon was too high a price to pay for anything the trap would produce. Nevertheless, Ryan was intent on testing the product of his effort. After placing the trap in a few feet of water on rocky bottom with some current running over it, he said to Neva, "That's where they live."

Neva laughed out loud and replied, "I'm more concerned with what they're eating than where they live."

The next morning Ryan pulled his trap in to find maybe ten large crayfish dining on the bait. As he carried them back to camp he realized that keeping them alive and fresh on the trail would be a problem and announced to Neva that she would soon be served a crayfish breakfast. After enjoying a hurried meal of boiled crustaceans, Neva was forced to admit, "OK, so your crayfish trapping is worthwhile, but you do need to scale it up a bit." Ryan was more than satisfied with her qualified approval.

Two days later the train crossed the Raft River, a tributary of the Snake, and passed the second intersection of the Oregon and California Trails. There were no defectors at this junction as all of the wagons that intended to leave the train to travel to California did so at the first Parting of the Ways. This branch of the California Trail went southwest, joining the main branch in present day northeastern Nevada. It then followed the Humboldt River west before reaching the Sierra Nevada mountain range in northern California. The California Trail was acknowledged to be the most arduous and demanding of all of the trails west in the days before travel by rail was possible.

The train was now traveling through the Snake River Basin, also known as the Snake River Plain, a relatively flat depression extending east to west almost 400 miles across all of what is now southern Idaho. The trail was a dry, dusty one along the steep banks and high cliffs that rose above the Snake River. The region received little rain and the waters of the Snake came mostly from the melting snow that fell in the surrounding Rocky Mountains. Although the river was never far off, there were no accessible sources of water and little in the way of food for the cattle and livestock. The days seemed endless along this dreary stretch of trail and

Captain Billy made them seem even longer by pushing the train as far as it could go each day. He reasoned that there was nothing to see or do but travel the trail, eat, and sleep and that shaving a day off this leg of the trip would be helpful later.

Driving Cattle across the Dusty Plains

(Original sketch in Oregon Trail Museum)

Four days after crossing the Raft River, the train arrived at Shoshone Falls, a spectacular waterfall over two hundred feet high. Just above the falls, the river narrowed and split into a series of rapids that flowed between islands of rock before cascading over a horseshoe-shaped rim that was more than nine hundred feet across. Known as the "Niagara Falls of the West", the falls was, in fact, even higher than its eastern counterpart. The train had to make a short side trip to camp near the falls, but this was a place for the emigrants to spend a little time sightseeing and get some extra rest and so Captain Billy felt the detour was justified. An early end to the day's travel was well deserved.

Almost everyone made the quarter mile walk to an overlook from which the full expanse of the falls could be seen and vivid details of the remarkable sight were eagerly recorded later that day by those keeping journals. Jacob Miller had been keeping tabs on Rambles since his recovery from the snake bites and decided to use the layover to call on him. "Can I take Rambles to see the falls?" he asked Captain Billy.

"Sure. Just keep him away from the edge," Billy replied.

With time to spare, Jacob thought a hike to a higher vantage point would offer a better view and he and Rambles clambered up a rocky slope well away from the others. After about fifteen minutes, however, the climb became a tiring one and Jacob realized that the view was not improving, just becoming more distant. As he turned to Rambles to admit his mistake, he saw Rambles frozen in place and making a low, slow growling sound. Less than twenty feet away a mountain lion with back arched and lip curled was staring back at Rambles, waiting for him to make a move.

Apparently, the two hikers had approached the spot where the lion was resting with enough stealth to surprise him and left the cat, hemmed in by rocks on all sides but one, with no place to go but past them. Jacob ended the standoff immediately by retreating as fast as he could while shouting at Rambles to do the same. Since mountain lions generally avoid such confrontations unless hunting for food, it was fortunate that the big cat saw Rambles more as a threat than a meal. As he stumbled down the hillside, Jacob was hoping that Rambles would see things the same way.

He did and followed Jacob's lead, but not without one eye on the cat until it was well out of sight.

Back at the campsite Billy asked how the walk went. Still trembling a bit and knowing that Rambles could tell no tales, Jacob downplayed the closeness of the call with the casual reply, "OK. We did see a cougar." Billy naturally assumed it was from a great distance.

Later that night as the cowboys were finishing dinner, Jesse suggested to the others, "Let's play a little poker tonight. It's been awhile." The stakes in this game were never high enough to affect anyone's future, but the bragging rights that went to the winners were painful enough for the losers to bear that the game was taken seriously by all.

After completing his evening rounds, Captain Billy joined the circle as the first hand was being dealt and said, "Deal me in." When Billy lost, he lost his own money, but when he won, it came out of the cowboys' pay and was a benefit to all of those who had a stake in the herd of cattle. Billy seldom lost.

It was the first such game that Dewdrop had attended and Jesse won the first hand with Dewdrop sitting close by his side. Jesse also won the second hand and, stroking Dewdrop's head, said to her, "You're good luck girl."

Before the next hand was dealt, one of the cowboys pulled an enticing hunk of dried meat from the group's larder and said, "Here Dewdrop, this is for you." She quickly took the bait and abandoned Jesse for the treat. Jesse thought little of the move until Dewdrop's new friend won the hand and the sizable pot that went with it. Making the win more memorable was the fact that he drew the only card in the deck that made it possible against very long odds.

"Why did you stay in that hand?" Jesse asked.

"I had faith in the dog," the winner said as he raked in his winnings. Playing now with one hand resting on Dewdrop's head, the same fellow won the next hand as well. A second cowboy tried the same thing and succeeded both in tempting Dewdrop to his side and winning the hand dealt after she came to him. Soon everyone was trying to coax Dewdrop to their side and the "friendly" game of cards erupted into a heated, six man fracas.

"That's it. Game over," Billy announced and the game ended there and then. The boys were still bickering as they prepared for bed and Dewdrop drifted away to find a quieter spot to sleep. Billy knew it was ridiculous to think that Dewdrop had influenced the game, but couldn't help himself from figuring the odds of Dewdrop sitting next to every single winner.

Three days after leaving Shoshone Falls, the train approached two scenic waterfalls about five miles apart called the Salmon Falls. Captain Billy's forward observer located an acceptable campsite near the first of the two falls and that's where Billy signaled the train to stop for the night. The emigrants quickly learned how the falls got their name as there were perhaps thirty or forty Shoshone Indians fishing below the falls for salmon. Although Shoshone Falls represented the farthest point upstream that the strongest of the salmon reached in their annual spawning run,

Salmon Falls was a major obstacle below which many ended their run. As a result, the fish were thick in the waters below the falls in late summer and early fall. To reach this point, the fish had traveled nearly nine hundred miles, swimming upstream to elevations of more than six thousand feet above sea level on their migration from the Pacific Ocean to their birthplaces on the Snake River.

After tending to their animals and setting up for the night, John Marshall and Ryan Walsh hiked down to the spot where many of the Indians were fishing. Ryan, of course, had his fishing gear in hand. Halo and Angus, suffering from several long, boring days on the trail, were quick to follow them down a well-traveled path to the water. The fishing technique used by the Indians fascinated Ryan. Since the salmon were less interested in eating than in mating, the Shoshone caught them not with hook and line but by wading into the water and spearing those close to shore with long lengths of willow tipped with a sharpened elk horn. "I've got to make myself one of those," Ryan remarked. The Indians were equally fascinated with the two small dogs nosing through the fish guts for snacks, having never seen either of these two particular breeds before.

Ryan slid a few salmon eggs he found among the entrails lying near what appeared to be a central cleaning station onto his hook and swung the offering into a likely spot well away from the Indians. The salmon weren't interested, but the trout that followed them to feed on their eggs were. Salmon were an important source of food for the Indians at this time of year, but the abundance of the resource allowed them to trade the fish for goods carried by westbound travelers passing the falls as well.

John bartered for two salmon and Ryan caught several nice trout before they headed back to camp to present the fresh fish to the girls. Dinner was something special that night.

The next day the train passed near the second of the two falls, the Lower Salmon Falls, but continued along the south side of the Snake without stopping. The following day it arrived at the point where almost everyone that could cross to the north side of the river did so in order to follow the more favorable northern route to Fort Boise. It was known as the Three Island Crossing, one of the most dangerous crossings the train would make during its entire journey. The river was swift and the river bottom was rocky and very uneven at this location and, although the river was divided into four branches separated by three islands, only two of the three islands would be involved in the crossing.

If the river was unusually high, a choice had to be made between waiting days or perhaps weeks for the river to recede or taking an alternate route into Oregon along the southern side of the river. The southern route avoided two dangerous crossings of the Snake, but it was a hot and dusty trip along a sandy trail, a price most were not prepared to pay. For this reason, safety was often compromised at this crossing. The frequent tragedies that occurred here eventually led to the introduction of a ferry service in 1853, well after Captain Billy's crossing decision had to be made.

Fortunately, the river seemed reasonably negotiable at the time and Billy and his officers decided to ford the river the next day. Their plan, however, included several precautions. First, the river bottom would be surveyed so that a path which avoided any deep potholes or drop-offs could be charted. This required someone with two ropes tied around his waist to make his way across the river to gauge the water depth and bottom structure of the three branches of the river to be crossed. The ropes would be held by people on both sides of each leg of the crossing to keep the scout from being swept away from his line of travel. The ends of the trailing rope would then be secured to each shoreline as a guide to the safest path across that leg. Since the survey would involve frequent dips under the surface, Billy chose a strong swimmer for the job.

Equally important was the fact that the local Indians were on hand to lead the cattle and then the animal teams and wagons across the river. This solved the common problem of the leading cattle and oxen turning around in panic during the crossing and attempting to return to the near shore. The Indians were accomplished river rats that swam the river for fun and provided this service in return for goods carried by the emigrants for just this purpose.

Lastly, Billy wanted only a few wagons in the water at a time so that the manpower available could be concentrated on any problem that developed. The cattle and the cowboys would be the first to cross, then the larger wagons and animal teams, and finally the lighter wagons and smaller teams. Weight in this crossing was an advantage as the lighter wagons were those most likely to be overturned or swept away by the current. Everyone was a bit nervous that night and slept a little lighter than usual.

The Three Island Crossing as It Looks Today

The paths across the river were only about six feet deep, but the water was running so clear that the river seemed shallower than it actually was. With the help of the Indians, the cattle swam across without incident. They lost some ground to the current at each leg of the crossing, but entered the water near the upstream end of each of the islands and emerged before drifting beyond the downstream end. The larger wagons held the bottom for the most part and made the crossing with no loss of property or livestock. The smaller wagons were a different story. They tended to float and one of the first to cross overturned, but was pulled to shore before being swept away. Captain Billy saw the accident from his position on the near side of the river and immediately ordered the use of stabilizing ropes and additional manpower to further insure the safety of the wagons that followed.

When it came time for the Walsh wagon to cross, Ryan and Neva took their places on the bench seat and Angus stood peering out of the back of the wagon. Soon after entering the water, their wagon lurched abruptly to one side and Angus was tossed from his perch and into the water. In seconds the little dog was swept well downstream and, struggling to keep his head above water, was unable to bark a plea for help loud enough to be heard. Ryan and Neva's eyes were focused on what lay ahead and didn't see what had happened. It was a miracle that someone did and that someone was Captain Billy.

Billy was supervising the entry of each wagon into the river and was still looking at the back of the Walsh wagon when the mishap occurred. Rambles saw it too and was the first to react, turning and running along the river bank in Angus' direction. Billy hopped onto Bucket and was about to follow when a more critical situation developed. Another small wagon had overturned between the first and second islands and was free floating downstream, dragging its animal team under and impeding the escape of its occupants. One of the Indians on the far side of the river sprinted as fast as he could along the shoreline until he got ahead of the wagon and, timing his entry to intercept it, was able to free the animal team and lead it to shore. There was nothing he could do for the wagon's occupants as they were nowhere to be seen. Jesse was stationed on the far side of the river and was quickly galloping downstream as well.

Billy and Jesse both knew that they had only a few minutes to find the missing emigrants before they either drowned or were carried beyond the point in the river where they could follow on horseback. The river narrowed below the crossing, running faster as a result and making the rescue efforts even more difficult.

Riding on opposite sides of the river, Billy and Jesse reached the drifting wagon in less than a minute, but didn't see the people who went into the water with it. Billy shouted over to Jesse, "Ride downstream as far as you can and see if you can find anybody. I'll check the wagon." Although Billy knew it was very risky to do so, he and Bucket charged into the water. It was a struggle, but Bucket made it to the rolling wagon with Billy shouting repeatedly, "Is anyone in there?" His fears were realized when he heard the frantic screams of a young girl. "Get out of the wagon!" Billy yelled. The girl was able to crawl out of the back of the rolling wagon and tumbled into the water where Billy was there to grab her. How Bucket maintained his position treading water in the swift current without drifting away from or into the wagon would puzzle Billy forever, but somehow he managed it. "Is there anyone else in the wagon?" Billy asked.

Breathless and crying, she answered, "No. The others are in the water."

Squeezing the girl under one arm, Billy directed Bucket to the far side of the river which was now the closer side. Although the shoreline was rocky and much steeper than it was upstream, Billy found a way to maneuver the group to higher ground. He would wait there comforting the terrified girl until Jesse returned from his trip downstream.

At the same time Billy's rescue was taking place, Rambles was keeping his eyes glued on Angus and following his movement downstream even though he lost sight of him whenever the small dog was pulled underwater by the current. Angus was tiring and desperately gasping for breath when Rambles finally got well ahead of him and jumped into the water. The current was carrying Rambles along slightly ahead of and at the same speed as Angus, but he had to swim crosscurrent in order to reach the drowning dog. Rambles was nearly there when he saw Angus one last time before he disappeared for good below the surface. Rambles poked his head into the clear water and spotted Angus drifting lifelessly a few feet below him. He dove the short distance between them, grabbed Angus by the back of the neck, and somehow dragged him to the far shore.

Although the shoreline was only about twenty feet away, the two dogs were carried another hundred feet downstream before an exhausted Rambles finally reached it. Once they were out of the water, Rambles could only watch and wait, but it was only seconds before Angus coughed up some water and opened his eyes. After taking a few minutes to rest and recover, the two picked their way along a rocky shoreline, climbed up to level ground, and then walked wearily back to the crossing.

When Ryan and Neva reached the first island, Neva realized that Angus was missing and, fearing the worst, began crying. With tears streaming down her cheeks she could say only, "I should have watched him closer." When Ryan and Neva reached the second island, however, there was a pleasant surprise in store for them. Rambles and Angus were sitting upright on the far shore waiting for them to arrive.

Not quite believing his eyes, Ryan asked, "How did he do that?" Ryan and Neva would never know the whole story, but the reunion with their wet dog was an emotional one.

About thirty minutes later, Jesse rode up with a small body draped across the back of his horse's neck. Billy led him away from the girl and asked, "What's the story?"

Jesse reported, "I found the boy floating in the river and managed to pull him out. I saw no sign of his mother or father. I'm guessing they're far downriver by now."

With that Billy said, "OK. You ride ahead. I don't want the girl to see her brother this way." On the ride back, Billy was left with the task of explaining to the girl that her family was dead, drowned in the river, and assuring her that he would see to it that she was cared for properly. She would have wept if she were not still in shock.

All of the other wagons eventually made it across the river safely, but word of the casualties spread quickly and put everyone in a somber mood. That evening Captain Billy informed the emigrants that the train would not leave until noon the next day to allow those with wet supplies time to sort and dry them and, of course, to conduct a funeral service. Although only one body was buried, three wooden crosses showing the name, birth date, and date of death of each of those killed in the crossing accident were placed side by side at the gravesite. Because the survivor, an eight year old named Sarah, knew and liked Missy, the Marshalls agreed that she could travel with them until a permanent placement could be arranged. As planned, the train left the camp on the north side of the Snake around midday and headed northwest, away from the river, towards Fort Boise.

CHAPTER 9 - I ONCE HAD A TAIL

It was early August when the train left its campsite at the Three Island Crossing and headed northwest, away from the Snake River and directly toward Fort Boise. The fort was 130 miles and eight days travel away. Water was scarce for the first four days. The train was traveling through the northernmost part of The Great Basin, a high altitude desert where nighttime temperatures were often quite low even in the summer, forcing the emigrants to break out their heavy blankets for the first time. Elevations of 6000 feet above sea level were not uncommon and snow was a possibility at any time of the year. The cooler temperatures were a welcome change during the long days on the trail and the train covered more ground than usual along this stretch. The lack of water and good grasses, however, tested the stamina of the cattle and animal teams.

Sarah, orphaned in the Three Island Crossing accident, had become Missy's shadow and they walked the trail together each day with the little dogs discussing all things of interest to girls of their age. Missy avoided any mention of the accident, but Sarah was far from over it and worried constantly about her future. It was helpful that Halo and Angus were always there to divert her attention from her sorrow and fears and that the Marshalls and her inclusion in the evening play group gave her a sense of belonging that was lost at the crossing.

The day before the train was scheduled to reach Fort Boise, Neva Walsh stumbled over some rocks on the trail, fell hard to the ground, and injured her arm. Ryan helped her to her feet and asked, "Are you OK?"

"I think I've hurt my arm badly," she replied, grimacing in pain.

It was late in the day and so she soldiered on until the train made camp before summoning Doc Brookings. With a gentle feel and some pressing here and there, Brookings informed Neva that she had broken her arm, but that the fracture was not a serious one as the bone was only cracked and did not have to be reset. "Do you want a splint or a cast?" he asked her, explaining that a cast was probably the better choice for travel on the trail. Neva took his advice and the two walked to the supply wagon containing Doc's medical supplies. Doc carefully bandaged Neva's lower arm and wrist, mixed some gypsum powder with water to form a paste, and applied a thick layer of the paste to the bandaged areas. "This stuff will take time to harden so don't touch it to anything for a while," Doc instructed her. He didn't realize that he was holding her hand and staring into her eyes, seeing for the first time what a lovely young lady she was, but when the trance ended, he turned away to hide his flushing face and stated in a most professional manner, "Let me know if you have any problem with the arm." Neva returned to her wagon in a much better frame of mind.

Four days after crossing the Snake, the train came to the Boise River where it made camp for the night. For the next several days, the train would be moving along the south shore of the river through the relatively lush Boise River Valley. Water and grass were plentiful along this stretch of trail, giving the cattle and animal teams a chance to put on a little weight and regain some of their strength. The trail was smooth, there was little dust, and good campsites were easy to find. It was therefore a pleasant stretch of trail that provided comfort and relief to the weary emigrants as well. The train made a crossing to the north side of the river the day before reaching Fort Boise.

Established in 1834 on the Snake River by The Hudson's Bay Company to compete with Fort Hall for the fur trade, Fort Boise later became an important supplier of goods and services to travelers on the Oregon Trail. Unfortunately, the fort was in decline when Billy's train arrived as the trappers had decimated the beaver population to the point where the fur trade was now only a small fraction of what it was just five years earlier.

Billy was shocked to see the once thriving commercial center in a sad state of decay. The luxuries and sumptuous banquets offered to travelers by The Hudson's Bay Company in the past were now only memories. The fort would be abandoned completely a few years later as a result of river flooding and Indian attacks. Those counting on the fort for supplies were disappointed to find that, other than fish, little was available.

The Outside of Old Fort Boise Circa 1849

The Inside of Old Fort Boise Circa 1849

(Drawings from the 1949 report of Major Osborne Cross to the Quarter Master General)

Supplies for most of the emigrants were in fair shape, but for others the food they carried would have to be carefully rationed for weeks to come. Those who could bought some smoked salmon to supplement their food supply.

It had been more than a week since the emigrants last saw the Snake River, but they were now preparing to cross it again the next day. The river ran north-south at Fort Boise and would later represent the border between the present day states of Idaho and Oregon. The crossing was a treacherous one, but no worse than the first and, with the help of the local Indians and tricks learned along the way, both the cattle and the wagons made the crossing safely. The skill with which the young Indians guided the animals across the river was remarkable and impressed everyone on the train.

It was late in the day before the crossing was completed and the emigrants made camp for the night on the west bank of the Snake. Captain Billy spread the word that cholera outbreaks were being reported almost daily along the stretch of trail the train was now traveling and suggested that water be taken from all rivers and creeks as far upstream from riverside campsites as possible to minimize the risk of contracting the disease. He also reminded the emigrants that bathing in contaminated water was unsafe and that any water collected in slow running creeks needed to be boiled before drinking it. Having passed the graves of so many cholera victims along the trail, everyone took his warnings seriously.

The next morning the train left the river behind and headed northwest in the direction of the Blue Mountains. The trail was again hot, dry, and dusty and any uncovered necks were caked with dust at the end of the day. The morning after leaving the Snake, the train began a slow ascent to the summit of Keeney Pass. The trail through the pass was not a particularly steep one, but the steady climb and summer heat proved exhausting for the animal teams. The train camped for the night on the far side of the pass and the next day came to and crossed the Malheur River before stopping for the night. The campsite was a pleasant one and Captain Billy gave the emigrants some extra time the next morning to relax and recuperate.

Several evenings had passed since Dewdrop and Rambles last visited the Marshall campsite to fraternize with Missy, Halo, and Angus, but they were in a playful mood on this day and decided to join the festivities once again. They found that the addition of Sarah doubled the number of belly rubs and pets they were likely to receive. Ryan Walsh announced he was going fishing and reluctantly allowed the entire pack to follow him to the river. He now carried three weapons into battle - his fishing pole, his crayfish trap, and a newly constructed salmon spear. Unfortunately, there were no salmon running in the Malheur and his chance to spear one would have to wait. The bite would certainly have been better if the dogs were not jumping in and out of the water wherever he tried to throw his line. "Missy, keep the dogs out of the water," Ryan pleaded, but his request was beyond Missy's control and he managed only to set his crayfish trap before returning to camp empty-handed.

"Where's all the fish?" John Marshall asked.

"Ask your dog," Ryan replied.

"Bacon and beans coming up," Neva announced.

Two days after crossing the Malheur, the train was reunited with the Snake River for the third time, but would not have to cross it again.

This point was known as Farewell Bend because it marked the last time the emigrants would see the Snake after following it for over three hundred miles. Captain Billy called the train to a halt to make camp near the river in midafternoon. The next day the train would begin the demanding and dangerous climb through the Burnt River Canyon and the extra time would allow the emigrants to prepare for the ordeal in their own ways. The trip through the canyon was expected to take about five days.

Tilted Trail in the Burnt River Canyon

Negotiating the canyon was difficult at best and almost impossible at worst. The trail was rocky and uneven, perhaps the worst of the entire journey, meandering from one side of the creek that ran through the canyon to the other when it was not tilting the wagons sideways on the steep mountainsides surrounding it. In many places the uphill side of the wagons had to be held down by the weight of several men moving from wagon to wagon and it was often necessary to chop through the brush and brambles along the banks of the creek to clear paths for the many crossings. Billy was following the path taken by earlier trains as closely as possible to take advantage of their trail blazing efforts.

The Burnt River got its name from the blackened hillsides that bordered it, the result of frequent grass fires thought to be set by the local Indians. The Indians found that the new growth of grass following a fire was stronger and greener than that which was burned. Reports of heavy smoke in the canyon by those traveling through it were common, but no fires were burning and the air was clear during the passage of Billy's train. Since there was little open space to camp, the emigrants spent all but one of the nights in the canyon in a single line along the trail. In this configuration the train's usual security measures were impractical and everyone assumed some responsibility for guarding their livestock against thievery by Indians. Horses, in particular, had to be watched carefully, as they were the targets of most of the theft attempts.

On the second day in the canyon, one head of cattle and an oxen gave out. The cowboys believed that the cow was sick and, without knowing what disease it died of, dragged it to the side of the trail and left it for the buzzards. The oxen, on the other hand, died of simple fatigue and was butchered for an evening roast that fed the entire train, including Dewdrop and Rambles. The first of the four oxen saved at the Three Island Crossing replaced that which provided the evening meal.

The next day Doc Brookings was called to the wagon of a middle aged couple who had fallen ill. Doc wasn't sure of their illness, but the symptoms were similar enough to those of cholera that he treated them as if cholera was the cause. Too sick to walk the trail they were placed in makeshift beds inside their wagon and Brookings himself led their team forward, stopping often to let one or the other take care of business outside of the wagon.

For the next twenty four hours Doc left them only to eat. The following day they both seemed stable, if not recovering, and Brookings concluded that they were suffering from food poisoning and dysentery, not cholera, and that his constant attention was no longer needed. Captain Billy assigned one of the cowboys to manage their wagon until the couple were well enough to travel on foot. It would be another two days before that was possible. Billy also issued a strong warning that any water from the shallow, slow flowing creek was not to be trusted as the effluent produced by the trains ahead would surely be funneled into it by the steeply sloping adjacent shorelines. Ryan Walsh would be doing no crayfishing in this creek.

The train spent the fourth night in the canyon strung out along a narrow stretch of trail. Physically exhausted, the emigrants did little socializing and were in bed soon after dark. Dewdrop chose a comfortable spot next to one of the supply wagons at the head of the train to curl up for the night. Because the wagon sat on a gentle slope with the oxen still hitched to it, Captain Billy chocked the wheels with rocks to keep it from moving during the night. His precautions, however, were not enough to keep the oxen from pulling the wagon just a foot forward as Dewdrop slept with her tail snugged under one of the wheels. The steel rim of the wheel which bore the weight of the heavy wagon rolled onto and then over Dewdrop's tail, crushing it close to its base. The intensity of the howling and yelping that followed aroused everyone and Jesse and others lying nearby were soon at the scene to see what was going on. There they found the poor girl dancing in circles in anguish, her tail bent at almost a right angle at its thickest part. "She broke her tail!" proclaimed Jesse, "but how?" By the light of a lantern Jesse detected a slight rocking of the wagon as the oxen shuffled back and forth and that provided the clue needed to answer his question. "That's one wagon accident I didn't figure on," he declared.

While onlookers tried to console Dewdrop, Doc Brookings got the call and arrived a few minutes later to offer medical assistance. He quickly concluded that the tail had to come off. "I need some things from the wagon. You get some water hot," Doc instructed Jesse.

A few minutes later Doc returned with his surgical instruments, some bandages, a container of alcohol, and a bottle of chloroform. Only a year or two earlier, two chemicals were used for the very first time as general anesthetics. One was ether, a cheap and simple way to eliminate pain and safer for the patient than chloroform, but it was slow to take effect and, more importantly, was a highly volatile and potentially explosive liquid if exposed to heat or light. It was not to be used in hot, dry climates. For this reason, Doc decided to carry chloroform. Although it was more toxic than ether and produced heart failure and death in some early cases, it was fast acting and didn't pose the explosion danger that ether did. Neither of the two is used today as a general anesthetic.

132

Brookings had little experience with either chemical, but reasoned that if an anesthetic was needed, the risks associated with chloroform would have to be taken. Unsure of the proper dosage for a dog, he placed only a few drops on a cloth and covered Dewdrop's face. She was out in seconds. The surgery was a simple one and when it was over Dewdrop's tail was only a stub about an inch long. A few of the cowboys watched the procedure. The others were too squeamish to watch and walked a short distance away until the deed was done. "Does anyone want a souvenir?" Doc asked as he held twelve inches of cartilage and hair up for all to see.

"I do," Jesse replied, although he had no idea at that moment exactly what he would do with it.

Dewdrop was slow to wake up and Brookings, worried that the dose of chloroform may have been too much, checked her heart continuously until she finally opened her eyes. Dazed as she was, Dewdrop sensed that her agony was over and the sting of a minor wound was all she would have to bear. She was sleeping peacefully well away from the wagons just an hour later.

The canyon also became the last stop for a pair of mules traveling side by side that collapsed from exhaustion late on day five in the canyon. Since no one had reached a point where mule meat seemed appetizing, the two were mercifully shot and left behind for the local scavengers, but not before the cowboys quickly filled a sack with some meaty shanks for the dogs. Two of the three remaining oxen saved at the Three Island Crossing were donated to the wagon that lost the mules.

Jesse and the cowboys took unusual care to roast the mule shanks just so before presenting maybe five pounds of meat on a huge thigh bone to each of the two dogs waiting patiently for dinner to be served. Rambles and Dewdrop were surprised to find that it was all for them and they soon entered into a glutton's heaven. Watching them eat, one of the cowboys wondered if their treat tasted as good as it looked and took a small bite of the next shank to come off the fire, one that was to be shared by Halo and Angus. "Hmmm. This ain't bad," he commented to the others and took a second and then a third bite.

"Yes, but is it good?" Jesse asked.

The others weren't waiting for an answer. "Let's cook it all," one said and the entire contents of the "dog" sack was soon hanging over the campfire. They enjoyed the mule as much as Dewdrop and Rambles did, but swore among themselves to keep their dinner that night an untold secret.

While his mule meat was roasting, Jesse carried a generous portion of the cooked meat to the Walsh and Marshall wagons for Halo and Angus. Both families and the dogs were sitting around their dying campfire when Jesse arrived. "I've got something for your dogs," he announced and handed the meat over to Missy to distribute.

After thanking Jesse, Missy asked, "Is there anything I can do for you in return?"

"Yes, there is. Sew Dewdrop's tail to the back of my hat, Davy Crockett style. I want to keep it wagging as long as I'm around," he explained. His request gave everyone but Missy a good chuckle. She

134

didn't see the humor in such a sweet gesture. The next morning Jesse joined the others shaking his head from side to side to show off his strange tribute to the dog. Dewdrop noticed the adornment too, but didn't recognize it as hers and so was unimpressed. She was still getting used to the bandaged nub that she could wiggle, but not wag.

After finally leaving the Burnt River Canyon and its miseries behind, the train traveled over an arid expanse of land known as Virtue Flats. The trail was smooth and straight and the train covered more ground in one day than it did in the previous five in the canyon. Miles of wagon ruts on these flats can still be seen today. Although there was no water on this stretch of trail, there was plenty of grass and the cowboys allowed the cattle to fall behind to give them more time to graze.

Crossing Virtue Flats

Later that day the train came to Flagstaff Hill, a high point on the trail where the emigrants got their first glimpse of the Blue Mountains in the distance. They were now entering the Baker Valley, an area formed by the Blue Mountains and the Elkhorn Range to the west and the Wallowa Mountains to the east. Good grazing, clean water, and plenty of firewood would be available to them for the next few days. The tens of thousands of emigrants passing through the valley were unaware that a decade later gold would be discovered in the neighboring hills and that Baker City, a town that didn't exist when Billy's train made camp there for the night, would become the center of a thriving mining economy soon after the discovery.

CHAPTER 10 - SUMMER SNOW

After traveling through the fertile grasslands of the Baker Valley and crossing several beautiful creeks, the train arrived at the Powder River, a winding tributary of the Snake River and the gateway to the Grande Ronde Valley. The crossing was an easy one and the emigrants were making camp on the north shore only a few hours after reaching the river. With a few hours of daylight remaining, Ryan Walsh was anxious to try his luck on the river, but this time he planned to sneak off by himself to avoid the riverside commotion created by the children and the dogs. He whispered to Neva, "I'm going fishing. Keep the dogs and the girls here."

"OK," she replied, "But don't be long. I need to start dinner soon."

Once he reached the river, Ryan walked along the bank looking into the water for signs of fish when he saw several salmon swimming upstream in search of their birthplace. "At last," he thought, "a chance to use my new spear." He excitedly moved ahead of the fish to a shallow spot where they were likely to pass, quickly removed his boots and socks, and waded into the water with his spear raised above his head. As the fish swam within a few feet of his position, he struck, but missed. He plunged the spear into the water again and again as the fish quickly moved away, but still came up empty. The chase upstream lasted only a few seconds before the fish were well out of range. "What am I doing wrong?" he asked himself. He then realized that the apparent position of the fish was being affected by the refraction of light at the surface of the water and that he needed to adjust his aim to correct for it. The Indians had learned this lesson long ago. Not one to give up easily, Ryan returned to the shoreline and raced upstream to get ahead of the fish once again. He was successful on his second attempt and then again on his third and fourth.

After cleaning his catch and setting his crayfish trap, he returned to camp with three nice salmon. "Here you go, Neva. I'll let the Marshalls know there's fresh fish for dinner," he declared proudly. What Ryan did not know was that the floor of the Powder River was littered with gold, enough to lure hundreds to the river to pan for the precious metal just a few years later, and that he may well have stepped on and over enough of it to have solved all of his money problems.

It was still early evening when Doc Brookings walked to the field where the cattle were grazing to check on Dewdrop. The cowboys were off collecting firewood and Dewdrop and Jesse were preparing a fire pit when Doc arrived. "How's she doing?" Doc asked as he examined her bandaged stub.

"I don't think she misses it much," Jesse replied, draping her tail over one shoulder for emphasis. Captain Billy and Rambles joined Doc and Jesse a few minutes later. Rambles seemed more interested than usual in the area of Dewdrop's injury and politely sniffed it upon arrival. The two dogs playfully sprinted back and forth for a few seconds and then drifted off toward the cattle. "Stay for dinner, Doc," Jesse offered.

"OK. I'm free tonight," Doc replied. Although he occasionally ate alone, Doc typically received a dinner invitation from a different wagon each night. This was not only a convenience to Doc, but it provided the emigrants an opportunity to discuss their medical issues with him and to get to know him better in case they needed his help.

Travel the following day was even more pleasant than it was the day before. The train reached La Grande, a popular campsite for westbound travelers, in the late afternoon. This was a staging area where the emigrants prepared for their ascent into the Blue Mountains. Captain Billy met with his officers that night to explain to them that, although passing through the Rockies was difficult, getting up and over the Blue Mountains would be the most challenging obstacle the train would face during the entire trip.

Unlike the mountains the train had negotiated earlier, the Blue Mountains were covered with thick forests of stately pine and spruce trees, held many areas of good grass, and had abundant sources of water. The trail, however, was steep and rough and riddled with dangers. The highest peaks in the range stood at 9000 feet above sea level. As encouragement Billy added that, once the Blue Mountains were behind them, everything that lay ahead would seem easy by comparison. The Blues now represented the last major mountain range between the emigrants and their final destination.

During the night the temperature dropped to near freezing and the emigrants awoke to find the ground covered with a heavy frost. Missy Marshall complained to her parents, "It was so cold last night I had to hold Halo against my belly to stay warm."

"Well," replied her father, "we're pretty high up and you can see the snow on the mountain peaks. You'll have an extra blanket tonight." It took the train a little longer to break camp that morning, but it was on its way by 9 a.m.

The climb began as expected. The trail was rough and, at many points, the grade was so steep that the animals alone could not pull the wagons forward. The men and boys worked in groups, pulling the heaviest wagons and those with feeble animal teams up the steepest slopes with ropes, chains, and pulleys while the women and children followed behind, placing stones behind the wheels to keep the wagons from rolling backward. To make matters worse, a freezing rain had begun and staying warm and dry was now an additional concern. Captain Billy was unsure whether he preferred the trail icy or muddy since either condition would prove hazardous and slow the train down.

As the train made its way to higher elevations, the sleet turned to snow and by late afternoon the trail was covered with several inches of the white stuff. A strong wind soon became a part of the mix, blowing the heavy snow around and reducing visibility to only a few yards. In addition, it was no longer possible to step or steer around the rocks and potholes that were now hidden from view by the drifting snow. The weather was obviously getting worse rather than better and Captain Billy ordered an early end to the day's travel in the hope that the storm would pass and conditions would be better the next morning.

Once the wagons that had fallen behind and those helping them up the grade finally assumed their place in line, everyone was looking for somewhere to hunker down until the storm subsided. Those who had not slept inside their wagons since the hailstorm or emptied it at river crossings now sought the shelter of their canvas roof. With the women and girls already tucked inside their wagons, Ryan Walsh and John Marshall stood outside in the blizzard sizing up the situation. "It's still summer isn't it?" Ryan asked.

"Not up here," John answered. The conversation was a short one. After climbing into his wagon, John realized that, although it was larger than most, it was quite cramped with Emma, Missy, Sarah, Halo, him, and all of their supplies occupying it at one time.

"Where's my new buffalo coat?" Emma asked, rummaging through the pile of goods on which she sat. "I'll be needing it tonight."

Jesse and the cowboys were attempting to secure the herd with a makeshift corral since keeping a close eye on the cattle this night would be next to impossible. The two large supply wagons were positioned about fifty yards apart to block the trail on either side of the herd. The cowboys would use the supply wagons for shelter with one of them venturing out in the storm at intervals to insure that all was well. "There's no place for them to go," Jesse concluded, "and if any do drift away, they won't get far on this hillside and in this weather." Jesse helped Dewdrop up and into one of the supply wagons and Captain Billy and Rambles piled into the other. As Jesse looked for an unoccupied spot in his wagon, he said to his group, "No smoking. No farting. What's for dinner?" They shared a bag of jerky, drew matchsticks to see who would be going out on patrol later that night and when, and then tried to get comfortable in their crowded quarters.

They drew sticks a second time to see who would share Dewdrop's warmth on this bitter cold night. As the winner curled up next to her, the others heard him murmur, "Dewdrop my girl, please keep your fleas to yourself." They wondered if the winner might not be so lucky after all.

Sleeping practically on top of each other, the emigrants spent a long, restless night trying to stay warm, knocking the accumulation of snow on their roofs off from the underside, and occasionally peeking out through the canvas flaps at the ends of their wagons to check on the storm. It snowed all night and was still coming down, although less heavily, at daybreak. When Captain Billy and a few other hearty souls emerged in the morning to survey the situation, they found the snow to be well above the tops of their boots and, in places where it had drifted, several feet deep. Confident that no other trains would be coming up behind them until the storm passed, Billy decided to use the day to rest and regroup rather than attempt to move on.

The first order of business was building a fire. For those who normally ate a cold breakfast, it was the night before last since they had

142

had something hot to eat or drink. Jesse and the cowboys missed their coffee and were out before most clearing spots on the ground for community campfires and looking for firewood. An hour later they had three fires roaring along the length of the train. Soon after that the travelers were heating beans and bacon, boiling coffee, and discussing the storm that had stalled the train's progress.

Halo was up and moving around before the others in the Marshall wagon. Feeding her was not a priority the night before and so she was hungry. She woke Missy and Missy woke Sarah and so on. Once he was awake, John Marshall was anxious to know what the plan for the day was and left the wagon to find out. An hour later he returned with the news and a hot breakfast for Emma and the girls. Halo got only cold bacon for which she would have been grateful were it not for the fact that it was really cold, almost frosty and quite tasteless.

With the storm subsiding and bathroom duties overdue, Emma bundled Missy and Sarah up for the trip outside. The snow was above Missy's knees and, with a puzzled look on her face, she asked her mother, "How do we poop in the snow?"

"You'll have to figure that out for yourself dear," Emma replied.

Halo was resourceful and found a spot under the wagon where the snow was only a few inches deep to do her business. Emma was still wearing the splendid new winter coat she had slept in, one she had not envisioned needing until much later in the year. As she squatted behind a nearby clump of bushes, John shouted with a smirk, "You look stunning in buffalo, my dear."

Blizzard in the Blue Mountains

(Undated painting by Karl Ferdinand Wimar)

Emma knew that passing a twelve hour day in the wagon playing games to keep the girls occupied would seem like an eternity and decided to let Missy and Sarah play in the snow until they tired themselves out and, hopefully, were ready for a long nap. "Why don't you build a snowman?" she suggested and, with some help and instruction from John, the girls got busy on the project.

Halo was attempting to find an efficient way to move through the snow when Angus jumped from the next wagon to do his morning duty. He was not much taller than Halo, but used a high hopping technique to get around. Soon the two dogs were frolicking together in the snow, hopping around the site of the snowman under construction like rabbits, and occasionally disappearing in the snow for a minute or so to rest and catch their breath. Their day in the snow ended when the balls of ice that built up on the hairs between their toes became too large and irritating to ignore.

The snowman was not a large one, but it was well-crafted under Missy's exacting direction. With eyes and a mouth made of small rocks, a short stick for a nose, pine cones for buttons, and a pine bough for a hat, it drew compliments from all on the train who saw it.

By midday it had stopped snowing and the wind had dwindled to a mild breeze. Most of the emigrants spent the rest of the day gathering grass for their animals and catching up on the sleep they had lost the night before. The next morning everyone was anxious to leave the site, although no one was quite sure what to expect on the trail. The foot or so of early season snow that remained on the ground made travel all the more treacherous and walking through it would require more energy than many of the emigrants and animals had to give.

Captain Billy instructed Jesse to move the cattle ahead first, thinking they would trample a path the others could follow with less effort. It was slow going. The train slogged uphill for the rest of the day and, unable to reach the summit before dark, stopped for the night at one of the few wide and level spots in the area. While the first to stop were tending to their animals, the available men and boys continued to help the stragglers pull their wagons to the campsite.

The temperature was now rising and the snow was beginning to densify when the emigrants retired for the night. It was still not fit to sleep on the ground, however, and they spent yet another uncomfortable night nestled inside their wagons. Good grass lay below the melting snow cover and the hungry cattle and livestock were quick to nose their way down to it for some nourishment.

Early the next day, the train finally reached the highest point on its trek through the Blue Mountains. It would be downhill from here. The same techniques used to ascend the mountains would be needed on the descent to keep the wagons from tumbling down the trail or over adjacent cliffs. The descent was expected to be dangerous, but the slush and the mud beneath it was something Captain Billy had not anticipated. Halo and Angus were spared the hardship of walking on the sloppy trail and watched the operation from their usual positions in the Walsh and Marshall wagons. Although her herding skills were not needed on this day, Dewdrop moved with the cattle and the cowboys at the head of the train. Rambles followed Billy and Bucket as they moved back and forth along the length of the train checking on things. An early morning crust on the snow was particularly hard on Rambles' feet and his path through the slush was marked with traces of blood.

The trudge downhill was a slow one, but without incident until Billy heard several of the emigrants screaming for help. One of the wagons was sliding sideways off the trail at the worst possible place and those nearby could not completely halt the slide. Billy arrived only moments later to find the wheels on one side of the wagon hanging over the edge of a cliff and the wagon slowly slipping away. "Is anyone in the wagon?" Billy screamed.

"Yes, our son is!" came the reply.

Billy quickly dismounted, reached into the back of the wagon with one arm, grabbed the young boy by the coat, and lifted him off his seat in the wagon. At that moment the oxen team pulling the wagon could no longer hold their ground and stumbled over the precipice, dragging the wagon and the parents of the young boy along with them. The wagon free fell over a hundred feet to the bottom of the cliff. It all happened so fast that there was little the horrified onlookers could do. Two of them stood with outstretched arms that a second ago held ropes attached to the fallen wagon. Billy's adrenaline rush was so great that he held the boy of about four years of age in midair with one arm for much longer than he thought possible before lowering him to the ground.

Once the initial shock of the accident wore off, Billy had two of the younger cowboys come to the scene and, seeing that there was no way to reach the wagon on horseback, asked them, "Can you climb down to that wagon without killing yourselves?"

After mapping out a few possible paths to the bottom one of the two answered, "Sure," and the second agreed.

"Well, get down there and see if anybody is alive," Billy instructed them. Ropes were tied around the waists of the two as a precaution and twenty minutes later they had reached the wagon.

"They're both dead," one shouted up, "but two of the oxen are still breathing."

Doc Brookings had arrived just in time to find that he wasn't needed. Billy asked Doc to take the young boy away from the area and console him. At the same time, Billy was doing his best to keep all of the others attending to their business and away from the operation that followed.

Descent from the Blue Mountains

(1850 sketch by Cross)

The bodies of the two victims were secured to the ropes tied to the cowboys on their way down and dragged up the side of the cliff and onto the trail. The two surviving oxen were shot and killed. Although neither of the cowboys were experienced butchers, they managed to deal with all four of the fallen oxen by following instructions Billy shouted down to them. The meat was hoisted up the face of the cliff in sacks and later distributed to all who wanted some. Billy also asked the cowboys to rummage through the wagon and salvage the boy's clothing and any useful supplies and to send them up with food items that would help those on the train who were running low.

All of this took what was left of the morning and much of the afternoon. The train kept moving through it all, but at an even slower pace than before, and covered only a mile or so that day. It had been decided earlier to keep the cattle moving down the mountain and the herd was several miles ahead of the train by day's end. Getting the herd to greener pastures as quickly as possible was the objective and, for this reason, Jesse and the cowboys camped apart from the wagons for the first time. The cowboys that had helped at the scene of the accident rode up and joined the others just before dinner. Their delivery of perhaps fifteen pounds of fresh meat was a welcome surprise. It would have tasted better, however, if the details of the mishap that produced it were not the subject of discussion around the campfire. Among them, only Dewdrop ate well without feeling a bit of remorse.

Captain Billy decided that the muddy, rock-strewn trail on which the train now traveled was no place for a burial and delayed the funeral of the two unfortunate victims until a more suitable grave site could be located. The two would reside in one of the supply wagons until that time. The area where the wagon accident occurred later came to be known as

Deadman's Pass. Doc Brookings was busy trying to find a suitable wagon owner with whom the son of the deceased pair could finish the trip and, after talking to a number of candidates, was directed to a couple in their early thirties that wanted a child, but could not have one of their own. The interview went well and Doc could find no reason not to turn the boy over to the couple. "I think the child may have found a permanent home. Those people seem perfect," he told Captain Billy.

"How's the boy taking it?" Billy asked.

"He's too young to understand all that's happened, so it's hard to know. Let's see how he reacts at the funeral," Doc said, and then added, "You know Billy, he's the second young life you've saved on this trip."

Billy did not acknowledge Doc's comment and responded only by saying, "Let's eat."

The next day the train continued down the mountain and by midafternoon had reached a wider, flatter stretch of trail with little slush or mud on it. The cowboys and the cattle were five miles ahead of the train when they came to a large open area ideal for grazing and Jesse decided to make camp there to await the arrival of the others. It was early evening when the train finally rejoined the herd and, for the first time in days, the wagons circled for the night.

Captain Billy announced that the funeral would be held the following morning and instructed the cowboys to dig the graves. Billy himself made the markers. The open graves were waiting at sunrise and Billy conducted the funeral as soon as the emigrants had finished breakfast. It was attended by all but a few. Rambles sat upright at attention

150

at Billy's side during the entire ceremony. The son of the deceased couple was present, but showed little emotion. His caretakers told Doc Brookings that the boy had asked a lot of questions about the accident, but was unable to understand completely the loss of his parents. Doc reasoned that the swift transition to a new situation would help the boy avoid the trauma that an older child would certainly have suffered. The cowboys were still filling in the graves when the train broke camp. The cattle would again follow rather than lead the train. With the worst part of the descent now behind it, Billy hoped the train would have smoother sailing as its schooners headed west toward the Umatilla Valley.

CHAPTER 11 - WE ARE NOW ONLY THREE

It was early September as the train worked its way out of the Blue Mountains. It would camp one last time in the high country before making a gradual descent into the Umatilla Valley. Travel the day after the funeral ended at a campsite that was less than desirable, but with nothing better close by it would have to do. The train was still at an elevation of about 3000 feet. The emigrants had not yet finished unhitching their teams when an elderly man caught up with Doc Brookings for a consultation. Several fingers on the man's left hand were blistered and reddish black in color. After feeling his hand and fingers, Doc asked, "Where did you sleep during that cold night on the mountain?"

"In my son's wagon," the old man answered.

"Well, it looks like you froze your fingers that night," Doc replied. As the two walked to the wagon where Brookings kept his medical supplies, Doc gave the man treatment instructions and informed him that there was a chance of recovery, but that it would be several months before he would know if the fingers had to come off and, even if they didn't, there would be long term pain associated with his injury. Doc carefully cut away some of the blisters and bandaged the areas that needed it. "Come see me every week 'til we part ways and then see a doctor when you get where you're going," he told the man. Doc had little hope the dead fingers could be saved. Time would tell.

The evening was a chilly one, but that didn't prevent Missy and Sarah from playing with Halo and Angus once the Walsh and Marshall campfires were lit and dinner was cooking. Preoccupied with the difficult terrain and bad weather, Dewdrop and Rambles were unable to complete the pack of four since the trip through the mountains began, but showed up hungry on this evening to see if there was a handout to be had.

Missy noticed that the two larger dogs looked much thinner than they did when the trip began and, for the first time in several weeks, got the notion to collect scraps of food for Dewdrop and her companion. "Momma, please make the first contribution," she begged. Although she had no scraps, Emma acquiesced and produced some bacon to prime the collection pot. Missy was anxious to show Sarah how the charity was conducted and the two walked off with Missy chanting, "Passing the pot for Dewdrop." It was hard for all but the poorest of emigrants to dismiss the girls without adding something to the pot. The most pleasurable part of the exercise for Missy was hand feeding the food she collected to the dogs, a pleasure she was happy to share with Sarah. For their part, the appreciative dogs were mindful not to nip any small fingers in the process.

Once the dogs had been fed and the Walsh and the Marshall families sat down to eat, Rambles detected a faint, but familiar, sound, the howling of wolves some distance away. After a few minutes had passed, a second series of howls that were much louder than the first had everyone exchanging glances. Although it was just getting dark, a full moon was already high in the sky adding to the spookiness of the setting. It then became eerily quiet around the dying campfire as man and dog alike waited for the next set of howls to pierce the silence. When it came, it was so loud that it sent chills up everyone's spine. John Marshall nervously declared, "Those things can't be more than fifty yards away."

A short distance away Jesse and the cowboys were getting anxious as well. "They're comin' for the cattle," Jesse said, adding, "It's odd. They usually hunt quietly. Let's get out there before it's too late." Dewdrop wasn't waiting any longer either. She ran off toward the herd with Rambles close behind at about the same time Jesse and the cowboys were springing into action. Angus and Halo, unable to ignore the call of the wild, excitedly followed the big dogs into the twilight in spite of repeated pleas by Missy and Neva to stay put.

The cattle, alarmed by the nearby howls, were closing ranks when the cowboys reached them. Jesse and the others fanned out on foot to form a defensive perimeter around the herd, each of them peering into the twilight with a trembling hand resting on his sidearm. The wolves were now silent, hidden in their approach by clusters of large rocks on the hillside that bordered the grassy area where the herd was grazing. Searching for a weak and disoriented victim, the pack leader's slow, stealthy advance ended at a point only yards away from the nearest steer where he stood motionless, his breath visibly streaming into the chill night air.

Just as the attack was about to commence, Dewdrop and Rambles bounded into the space between the wolves and the cattle and began barking and growling in protest. Surprised, but in no way intimidated, the wolves simply made the dogs their first targets. Overwhelmed by the size, number, and ferocity of the wolves, Dewdrop and Rambles spun and danced in an effort to avoid the grasp of their deadly jaws. Angus and Halo stumbled into the fray only a second or two later and, before realizing they had come too far, also became prey. Small, black, and quick, Angus proved to be an elusive target. He did what he could to distract the pack from the defenseless Halo, but she was singled out almost immediately by the ravenous wolves, picked up by the back of her neck, and shaken hard.

The cowboys made their way to the fight scene within seconds and began shooting, easily distinguishing the dogs from their attackers in the bright moonlight. Once the first shots were fired the wolves fled, but not without Halo hanging limply from the mouth of the pack leader. One wolf lay dead at Rambles feet and a blood trail leading away from the scene indicated that at least one other had been wounded. "Good job, boys. I don't think they'll be back," Jesse remarked, but his thoughts were of Halo and how he would break the news of her fate to Missy. Dewdrop and Rambles sat wide-eyed and panting, each with bite wounds bleeding freely, but thankful, or as close to that as a dog can be, that the cowboys were there to end the attack.

The dogs had encountered a pack of Gray Wolves, also known as timber wolves. Gray Wolves were once common throughout Oregon, but they were hunted and trapped for their fur as early as the 1820s. Bounties placed on the species in 1843 led to a further reduction in their numbers. They were considered a nuisance and the bounties were intended to eliminate them altogether. There were probably only a few thousand left in the state by the time Billy's train passed their way. Headed by an alpha male and a breeding female, they live in packs that include pups and subordinate wolves of all ages. Their primary prey are elk, deer, moose, and bison although they will eat smaller animals and carrion if food is scarce. Howling is a form of communication commonly used to signal territorial possession to other wolves and can be heard as far as six miles away. The Gray Wolf thrived in a variety of habitats in which an adequate supply of food was available and once inhabited two thirds of the continental United States. By 1950 the Gray Wolf was extinct in the state of Oregon.

After reporting the details of the wolf attack to Captain Billy, Jesse made his way to the Marshall wagon to talk to John Marshall. John heard the commotion and shooting that took place less than a hundred yards away and, once he saw Angus return without Halo, was afraid that bad news was coming. After explaining to John what had happened, Jesse asked, "Do you want to tell Missy or would you like me to?"

"I'll do it," John replied.

Jesse was relieved that John would do the deed which he was dreading. Jesse stopped next at the Walsh wagon to tell Neva and Ryan of Angus' role in the story. Neva would have scolded Angus for his lack of obedience had she not been so relieved that he miraculously escaped the misadventure without a scratch. As Jesse left the Walsh campsite, he could hear Missy and Sarah sobbing loudly a wagon away, the sound of their sorrow he had hoped not to hear.

None of the wounds suffered by Dewdrop and Rambles were life-threatening, but Billy and Jesse led the pair to Doc Brookings to have a few of the uglier ones stitched up. After shaving around and suturing the worst of their wounds, Doc said aloud, "Those two are remarkable. They didn't even flinch."

"Doc, you have a way with dogs", Billy replied, "You should have been a veterinarian."

"Is that a compliment or an insult?" Doc joked. Brookings used the occasion to remove the last bandage that would be needed on Dewdrop's tail stub, commenting to Jesse, "The tail looks good. Short, but good. The end is even growing hair." Jesse responded only by gently stroking the length of that which hung from the back of his hat.

Early the next morning a funeral was held for Halo. It was attended only by the Walshes, the Marshalls, Sarah, Captain Billy, the surviving dogs, and a few of Missy's close friends and their family members. Missy, weeping throughout the service, gave the eulogy in which she referred to Halo as having gone from "her angel on earth" to an angel in heaven. As Missy spoke, Sarah held her hand as tightly as she could for support.

Everyone present had to hide or wipe away a tear or two at some point during the proceeding. John Marshall constructed a small cross with Halo's name on it and planted it close to the spot where Halo met her end. Dewdrop and Rambles sat respectfully through the short ceremony, occasionally licking the wounds they had received the night before. Although the purpose of the gathering was beyond his understanding, Angus was aware that Halo was missing and, in time, would come to know that he would never see his companion and playmate again.

Once the Blue Mountains were well behind them, the train entered the rich, well-watered Umatilla Valley, a pleasant area through which the emigrants were happy to travel and camp. Until 1845 the main trail passed the Whitman Mission, an outpost where travelers could receive medical care, purchase needed supplies, and trade with the local Indians. A shortcut that bypassed the mission was used by most westbound emigrants after 1845 unless the mission's assistance was needed.

The mission was established in 1836 by Dr. Marcus Whitman to provide religious instruction and medical care to the Cayuse and Umatilla Indians, but in late 1847 half of the tribe died in an epidemic of measles introduced by passing emigrants while the missionaries survived. The Indians blamed the deaths on the new religion, burning the mission to the ground and killing all who resided there. The shortcut became the main trail after that.

The train made camp at an ideal site in the heart of the Umatilla Valley the night of Halo's funeral. Competition for the best campsites was no longer an issue as all of those headed for destinations other than northern Oregon had already left the trail on which the train now traveled. Of the 50,000 or so emigrants that headed west in 1850, most ended up in California searching for gold. Only about 6,000 followed the Oregon Trail all the way to Oregon City.

The Whitman Mission

Once everyone had settled in for the night, Doc Brookings went to the Walsh wagon to check on Neva's broken arm. It had been almost a month since he first placed a cast on her arm and it was time to cut it away and replace it with a fresh one. "How does the arm feel?" Doc asked as he removed the last of the cast.

"Fine," Neva replied, "I have no pain at all."

Doc explained as he worked that she needed to wear the new cast for another month and that the growth of dark hair and stench of dead skin under the cast would be gone for good once it came off. Angus was watching the two intently, sniffing the discarded pieces of plaster and, when the official visit appeared to be over, danced before them to attract their attention. Without premeditation, Doc said to Neva, "Angus looks anxious. Shall we take him for a walk?"

Neva agreed and shouted to Ryan working nearby, "I'm going for a walk with Angus. I'll be back soon."

Ryan watched as the three disappeared into the nearby woods and wondered why Neva didn't mention Doc Brookings in her parting words. He would not have objected if she had. Later that night Neva mentioned to Ryan how nice a man James was. "Who is James?" Ryan asked. No one on the train except Captain Billy knew Doc Brooking's first name until that night. "I'd better ask Angus what went on out there," Ryan kidded. His words had the intended effect as Neva turned her blushing face away from Ryan's view.

The following day the train came to the Umatilla River and followed it downstream along the north bank that afternoon and all of the next day. The emigrants camped the second night at yet another beautiful and well-used site near the river known as Echo Meadow. The site was half a day's journey from the point at which the train would have to cross the Umatilla. That evening, after she had been fed, Dewdrop left the cowboys to visit the Marshall wagon as she had done many times before. This time was different, however. She found Angus laying listlessly near the Walsh campfire and Missy and Sarah sitting face to face next to the Marshall wagon. Although Sarah never mentioned the loss of her entire family in her efforts to console Missy, it was a fact that in some way helped Missy cope with Halo's death. Dewdrop stepped between the two girls, curled up at their feet, and closed her eyes. She was there to be petted as a comfort to Missy.

Early the next afternoon, the train crossed the Umatilla. The crossing was not a difficult one and the cattle and all of the wagons were across the river by mid-afternoon. Captain Billy ended the day early to give the emigrants a chance to prepare themselves for the dry and dusty stretch of trail ahead and to allow the cattle to eat and drink their fill.

The trip was wearing on Rambles, but he was rejuvenated by a late afternoon nap and decided to accompany Dewdrop on what had become a daily visit to the Marshall wagon. Missy and Sarah were growing quite fond of Dewdrop and, although her patches of bare skin and stitches were a reminder of Halo, she was proving to be an affectionate substitute over which the two could fawn. Rambles' presence on this day gave them each a dog to stroke, further improving their mood. Not to be forgotten, Angus trotted over from the Walsh wagon as soon as he saw the action develop to complete the reunion. It was not the same without Halo, but the three dogs were happy to be socializing together with the girls once more.

Ryan announced that he was going fishing and suggested to Neva that she invite Doc Brookings and the Marshalls to their wagon for a fish dinner. "And if you don't catch anything?" she asked.

"Just get them here by six with the fire going," he optimistically replied. As luck would have it, Ryan returned on time with enough trout and salmon to feed everybody, including the dogs. John Marshall brought along a bottle of fine whiskey he was saving for just such an occasion and a very pleasant dinner was had by all, particularly those of drinking age. Doc and Neva were seen casually holding hands more than once during the gathering, but no one dared to mention it.

The next day the train continued across the Columbia Plateau reaching Wells Springs, another popular camping area, where it stopped for the night. The day after that was a particularly long one. It was almost dark when the train made camp near the present day city of Arlington, the point at which some emigrants turned north toward the Columbia River to complete their journey by raft. Everyone on Billy's train, however, would remain on the trail at least until it reached The Dalles where the decision to continue by land or by river would finally be made. After breaking camp the next morning, the train made a gradual descent into a flat valley known as Alkali Canyon, a hot, dry, sandy stretch of trail strewn with rocks too large to easily be moved aside. The canyon was also notoriously windy and the wind-blown sand made travel a misery for both the emigrants and their animals. That night the train would make do at a campsite without wood or water and, once the sun had set, the temperature dropped precipitously, turning the sweltering heat of the day to what seemed by comparison to be bitter cold. It was an uncomfortable night for everyone.

The following day Captain Billy called the train to a halt in midafternoon. It was about to enter the Four Mile Canyon, the most difficult part of the trip across the plateau, and Billy wanted to avoid any problems that might arise by leading the weary travelers into the canyon late in the day. He also wanted to avoid the possibility that the train would slow to a standstill during the difficult ascent out of the canyon and be forced to spend the night strung out on a narrow and dangerous trail. The campsite was dusty and barren, but it was level and devoid of rocks.

Acting on the concerns of several of the wagon owners, Billy and the cowboys convened after dinner to discuss the condition of the herd and the wagon teams. Jesse reported that the cattle were in relatively good shape except for their feet. Many were now showing signs of worn and cracked hooves, heel erosion, and sole ulcers from the many miles traveled across hard and rocky terrain. Many of the mules and oxen were even worse off, hobbling along in distress and slowing the train down as a result. "Even Bucket needs a new a pair of shoes," Billy proclaimed, "but there's not much we can do out here. I'm hoping there's a good farrier or two at The Dalles." The group decided that any delay there insuring that the horses and wagon teams didn't break down before completing the trip would be time well spent for those continuing on by land. The cattle would have to go on as they were.

The train entered the canyon the next morning and by noon had begun the ascent up and out of its western end. It was a difficult climb, but no more so than those the emigrants had made before. Once the canyon was behind it, the train traveled another five miles before making camp for the day. The site was without amenities and the emigrants had to settle for either a cold supper or none at all. Many were now rationing their remaining supply of water as well.

Another two days and nights passed before the parched and exhausted emigrants completed the trip across the plateau and reached the east bank of the John Day River. A feeling of great relief came over everyone as the train made its way down a steep hill and the riverside campsite below came into view. It was a large and level site with ample firewood, grasses for the cattle and animal teams, and, most importantly, water. After four long, dry days on the plateau, the site appeared as an oasis to all that reached it. The debris scattered everywhere suggested it was occupied almost nightly. The location was known as McDonald Ford. Located only twenty miles from the point at which the John Day emptied into the Columbia River, it was where all westbound travelers crossed the river.

The next morning the train crossed the John Day. The cattle crossed first and the report from the cowboys was that the river was only about a foot deep and the river bottom was smooth and pebbly. Even Dewdrop's feet never once left the bottom. The crossing was therefore an easy one and took little time. After crossing the John Day, the train traveled another fifteen miles, winding its way through hilly terrain toward the Columbia River, before reaching the Deschutes River. It made camp on the east side of the Deschutes near its mouth to prepare for a relatively complicated and hazardous crossing the next day.

As usual, Dewdrop had dinner with the cowboys, but her normal ration of food no longer satisfied her hunger and she slipped away to the Marshall wagon for a little affection and something more to eat. She had learned that Missy was not shy about collecting scraps from others or raiding the Marshall larder in order to feed her, but even two dinners were not enough to satisfy her on some nights. Angus became an indirect beneficiary of Dewdrop's growing appetite, casually drifting over to the Marshall wagon during Dewdrop's feeding sessions for a handout.

That night Captain Billy and his staff had to choose between two very different ways of crossing the Deschutes. The first was to ford the river at its mouth by following the shallowest path across. The second involved crossing the river a short distance upstream at one of several points between rapids where the water was deeper, but slower than at the river's mouth. This required swimming the animal teams across first and then floating the wagons across. The river was nearly a hundred yards wide and the current was strong at each of the upstream crossing points. The women and children would be safely ferried across in canoes by the local Indians.

Since the water level was reasonably low, it was decided to ford the river at its mouth. The wagons would be driven out into the Columbia River on sandbars created by the flow of the Deschutes, entering the Columbia from its south shore, then make a wide circle around the mouth of the Deschutes, and finally turn back toward the south shore of the Columbia to exit the river on the western side of the Deschutes.

The Deschutes River Crossing

This could not have been accomplished without the help of the Indians who knew not only where the shifting shallows were at the time, but how to keep the cattle moving in the right directions once they entered the water. Although the crossing began early the next morning and went pretty much as planned, it was not until midafternoon that the last wagon reached the western side of the Deschutes. Relieved that the train had completed its last difficult river crossing without injury or loss of livestock, Captain Billy called it a day once everyone was across.

The emigrants were settled in by late afternoon and Ryan Walsh was not about to pass up the opportunity to use the extra time to go fishing. He had spent the previous evening thinking about the possibilities, but the train arrived at the east bank of the Deschutes with too little daylight left to leave the campsite. With pole in one hand and spear in the other and with Angus leading the way, he walked the half mile to the confluence of the Deschutes and Columbia rivers to try his luck. He was still looking for a promising spot when an unexpected arrival, Dewdrop, joined him and Angus on the river bank. Ryan thought it strange there were no Indians in sight and hoped their absence was not a sign there were no fish around. What he did not know was that the lower Deschutes was teeming with native trout. He was unaware as well that steelhead were making their spawning run from the sea and used the cooler and cleaner waters of the Deschutes as a stopover before continuing their migration up the Columbia to its tributaries and to the Snake River further upstream. Steelhead are the same species as the local rainbow trout except that they live in the sea and return to fresh water only to spawn. They also grow much faster and larger than a rainbow with mature fish weighing as much as thirty to forty pounds.

Ryan baited his hook, tossed it into a deep pool close to shore, and almost immediately caught a trout. While Ryan continued to pull smallish trout from the pool, Dewdrop drifted away to fish on her own. She found a shallow run not far from Ryan, studied it for a minute, and then slowly waded into the water. She had spotted much larger fish holding steady in the current and, once within striking range, began jabbing her head into the water in an attempt to grab one, albeit unsuccessfully. It took her a while to figure out how to land these fish, but she eventually did. She would herd them toward the shoreline only a few yards away and, once they were in water too shallow to swim freely, grab them in her mouth and deposit them on shore. She ate the best parts of the first, a steelhead of nearly eight pounds, before returning to the water for a second. Angus watched Dewdrop for a time and tried to copy her technique, but he succeeded only in making her job more difficult by scattering the fish.

Once Ryan noticed what Dewdrop was up to, he abandoned his effort and stole two nice steelhead from her once they hit the ground. By the time she was done, Dewdrop had stuffed herself with fresh fish and was fishing for the fun of it. She didn't miss those Ryan took for himself. As Ryan approached the Walsh wagon, Neva saw that the sack he was carrying was a heavy one and said to him, "I guess the fishing was good. I'll get the fire going."

"So good, in fact, that I was outfished by a dog," was Ryan's sheepish response. Anticipating dinner, Angus sat patiently waiting for his share of the catch which he preferred roasted rather than raw.

With her belly full and tired from a busy day, Dewdrop skipped her evening visit to the Marshall wagon to rest instead with the cowboys. As she curled up near the campfire, Jesse looked at her and said "Ah, there's nothing like the smell of a warm, wet dog." His comment did not disrupt her contentment.

After leaving its campsite on the western side of the Deschutes, the train traveled along the south shore of the Columbia, passing over a high ridge near midday where the emigrants got their first glimpse of the magnificent Columbia River Valley below and Mount Hood on the western horizon. It was a sight they had waited months to see, reminding them of the reasons they began the trip west. Later that day the train would reach The Dalles, the settlement where, until 1846, the trail ended and wagons were disassembled or sold and goods and supplies were transferred to rafts or riverboats at the mouth of Chenoweth Creek, a protected harbor nearby, for the seventy mile trip down the Columbia to the Sandy River or to Fort Vancouver another fifteen miles downriver. Dalles is the French word for "slabs", a reference to the sheer cliffs between which much of the Columbia River runs.

Prior to 1846 a reliable land route over the Cascade Mountains didn't exist and the treacherous water route down the Columbia represented the only option for completing the journey to Oregon City. Women and children floated downriver with their wagons while the men and boys drove the cattle and livestock single file along a narrow, cliff side trail that followed the river. The livestock had to cross the river twice, first to the north side at the Hood River and then later back to the south side at the Sandy, to complete the river route.

The Columbia, the largest North American river that flows to the Pacific, was swift and dangerous with many rapids, the longest and steepest of which was known as the Cascades. To bypass the Cascades, it was necessary to unload everything from the boats above the rapids, portage the goods overland for several miles, and then reload everything back onto boats below the rapids. Wagons taking the river route were reassembled at either the mouth of the Sandy River or at Fort Vancouver for the short land journey out of the Columbia Gorge and into the Willamette Valley. Many lost their lives moving their goods and animals down the Columbia.

Rafting Down the Columbia River

In 1846 a land route called the Barlow Road was established. It allowed travelers for the first time to pass over the Cascade Mountains and, although the western descent was dangerous, it represented a reasonable alternative to the river route. The river route was faster, but at a cost of $50 per wagon, it was expensive unless travelers built their own rafts and it involved back breaking portages around impassable rapids. Long waits for commercial rafts were also common and it was not unusual for strong fall winds to sweep up the river gorge, countering the river current and stalling the rafts on the water for long periods of time. Steamboats and portage roads would make the river route a more reasonable choice in later years, but these conveniences were not yet available in 1850. For those who chose the water route, Fort Vancouver became an important waypoint at which exhausted emigrants with no money were provided food, lodging, and even credit for needed supplies. Established in 1824 by the Hudson's Bay Company as a British fur trading post, the fort was later run by Chief Factor John McLoughlin who, although instructed by his superiors to discourage American settlers for business reasons, was particularly charitable to emigrants in need and was personally owed thousands of dollars at the time of his death in 1857.

Captain Billy and Rambles moved well ahead of the train as it approached The Dalles to secure a campsite and found those closest to the settlement already occupied. It was not unusual for five or more trains to be stacked up at The Dalles as it was the last place emigrants choosing the land route could purchase supplies and services and it was the staging area as well for those deciding to complete the trip by water.

The Dalles was also the place where relief expeditions organized by compassionate residents or charitable organizations met starving and destitute emigrants who had run out of food and money or lost their wagons and belongings before reaching The Dalles. The relief missions provided these unfortunate travelers with the assistance they needed to complete the last leg of their journey to the Willamette Valley. Captain Billy was thankful that no one on his train yet required outside help, but many arriving at The Dalles did, and they were forever grateful that it was available when it was most needed. After backtracking a bit, Billy waited for the train to reach him and directed it to a nice site only a mile short of the settlement.

Billy and his officers had waited until the train reached The Dalles in order to base their decision to proceed by land or water on the conditions that existed upon their arrival. The group had already dealt with all of the perils they would likely encounter on the land route and needed a good reason not to go that way, but had none, and unanimously decided to finish the journey by land. The group had come to trust Captain Billy's judgement completely and, for that reason, his was the only vote that really counted. No one on his train chose to part ways at The Dalles to complete the trip by water.

The train spent two nights and the day in between at its campsite near The Dalles. Captain Billy located a farrier, a trained hoof specialist, the evening the train arrived and arranged for him to spend the next day shoeing the horses that needed it most and treating the feet of the mules and oxen that were in the worst shape. The farrier was a good one. He gave the cowboys and others assisting in the effort a few quick lessons so that they could do the routine cleaning and filing of damaged hooves under his supervision while he took on the more delicate work of shoeing horses. This allowed all of the work that could not wait to be completed in one very long day.

The cost of the service was high, but it was paid for out of the train's common fund so that even those with little or no money were able to provide some care for their animals. The farrier reported to Billy that the problems he saw were the result of poor nutrition and too many miles on hard, dry trails and that most of them would disappear once the animals resumed a normal existence. After thanking and paying the man, Billy

172

walked over to Bucket and announced, "Sorry, boy. You'll have to wear your old shoes another few weeks."

Bucket gently pawed at the ground in response as if to say, "No problem, I can wait."

The day did not pass, however, without one serious mishap. One of the cowboys was working on the rear hoof of a mule when the mule pulled his leg away and kicked the cowboy in the head. The man dropped stone cold to the ground and was not moving when Jesse got to him. "Is he dead?" Jesse asked.

"No. I think he's still breathing," answered another with his ear to the injured man's chest.

"Go get Brookings," Jesse ordered. When Doc Brookings finally arrived the onlookers were throwing water on the unconscious man's face in an attempt to revive him.

"Don't drown the man," Doc said as he pulled a vial of smelling salts out of his bag. The inhaled ammonia did the trick and the downed man's eyes were soon open, but they were unfocused and a little crossed. Conscious, but unable to do more than stammer senselessly, the man had obviously suffered a serious concussion. After bandaging the wound on the back of his head, Doc instructed the others to find a comfortable resting place where the man could recover. Doc told them that rest was the only cure and that it might be several days before he could rejoin the others. "He is not to work without my OK," Doc sternly warned the injured man's associates, knowing these fellows were not ones that followed instructions well.

The Marshalls used the free day at The Dalles to walk into town and do a little shopping. Although there were no necessities on his list, John wanted to buy a few things he hoped would make the last leg of the journey more pleasurable. The Walshes made their way to the riverfront where they watched rafts being loaded for the trip downriver and Indians fishing for steelhead and salmon along the river's overhanging banks.

It has been estimated that somewhere between twelve and sixteen million fish swam into the Columbia River system from the sea each year before the settlers began their migration west. Salmon were the cornerstone of local Indian life and had served as the foundation of their culture and economy for thousands of years. In an effort to preserve the tradition, the first Columbia River fishing treaties were signed five years later in 1855. In these treaties, the tribes living near the river gave up most of their land, but reserved the right to fish the Columbia as they always had. The treaties were intended to allow the native people to remain fishermen rather than becoming farmers or laborers. In this way, they could continue to support and feed themselves, thereby saving the government the cost of their welfare. The dams and overfishing that came later would change all of that. The emigrants went to bed that night dreaming not of the two difficult weeks ahead, but of the end of the journey that would come in that time.

CHAPTER 12 - THE JOURNEY'S END

It was early Monday morning, September 16th, when the train left The Dalles. The cowboys and the cattle led the way, but the group had a slightly different look as its march along the trail began. The night before Captain Billy and Jesse came up with the idea of recruiting Jacob Miller to replace the cowboy sidelined by the mule until he was able to return to work. After all, his horse was now without a rider and Jacob would probably jump at the chance to escape the monotony of the daily walk on the trail. After first receiving approval from his parents, Jesse approached Jacob with the offer. Jesse explained to him that the job was only temporary and, although he was welcome to eat and sleep with the cowboys while it lasted, he might be more comfortable returning to his family each evening. It was up to him. Excited, but apprehensive, Jacob hesitated for a moment before admitting the obvious, "I don't know a thing about herding cattle."

"Well, if you want to learn, here's your chance," Jesse replied. Jacob nervously muttered a few words which Jesse took to be an acceptance. "OK then. See you first thing tomorrow. Don't be late," Jesse responded. With his heart racing, Jacob was worried more about getting to sleep that night than being late in the morning. On the walk back to his campfire, Jesse recalled the hazing he received in his first days as a rookie and hoped Jacob could handle the ribbing that was sure to come.

The next morning Jacob was waiting at sunrise near the cowboys' sleeping area for Jesse to get up and pull on his boots. While the coffee was cooking, Jesse laid out a simple plan, telling Jacob, "Today you'll ride with me. I'll teach you what you need to know and tomorrow you'll take your place in the herd. Don't' worry. I'll have Dewdrop keep an eye on you." The implication that a dog knew more about the job than Jacob was intentional.

Following the trail south toward the Tygh Valley, the train crossed a number of small creeks before making camp at a comfortable site with plenty of wood and clean, flowing water. Jacob chose to eat and sleep with the cowboys. The experience was relatively primitive compared to evenings with his family as Jesse had warned, but Jacob was more interested in camaraderie than comfort. He turned out to be a good sport as well, enduring the pranks played on him without embarrassment or complaint. It was all a welcome change. Captain Billy made it a point to stop by to make sure the cowboys had not already sent Jacob packing and was pleased to find that all was going well. Rambles hadn't seen his former nurse in some time and greeted him enthusiastically, raising his front paws to Jacob's shoulders and giving him a big lick on the face.

The next day the trail turned to the west into the heart of the valley and, at that point, Captain Billy halted the train early to provide the emigrants an opportunity to trade with the Tygh Indians. The Tygh were a small tribe, one of four that made up the Terino People, all of whom occupied territory in north-central Oregon. They were nomadic, spending summers along the upper stretches of the Deschutes River and winters in the Tygh Valley. Relying on hunting, fishing, and gathering for their subsistence, they did not engage in agriculture or the raising of domesticated animals. The Tygh were decimated by disease and warfare during the colonization of the west and no longer exist as a distinct tribe. The few that survived were forced to merge into other Oregon tribes.

Many of the Tygh were camped along the trail at the best locations in order to facilitate trade with the emigrants. One did not have to walk more than a hundred yards to meet with an Indian trader and many of the emigrants did at least a little window shopping once the train had settled in for the night. Dried berries and nuts were popular items and went well with the smoked salmon that many had purchased just two days earlier at The Dalles. It was a pleasant evening for most. Doc Brookings reported to Captain Billy that the injured cowboy was still a little shaky and that it would be another day or two before he could return to work. Later that evening, Billy caught up with Jesse and told him, "I don't expect any trouble, but double your watch on the herd and the horses tonight." Having survived his first day working alone as a cowboy, Jacob Miller would now find out what it was like to lose half a night's sleep while on watch.

The train followed the north shore of the White River, a tributary of the Deschutes, for two days after leaving the Tygh Valley and before arriving at the Barlow Gate, the only toll on the Oregon Trail at the time. The gate was named for Sam Barlow, the man who searched for and found a break on the southern shoulder of Mount Hood four years earlier and, with the financial help of Philip Foster and a crew of forty men, constructed a road across the Cascade Mountains. Barlow filed a petition with the territorial Assembly to make it a toll road and was granted the right to collect $5.00 per wagon and ten cents per head for all horses and livestock from those passing the gate.

Barlow collected the toll personally from 1846 to 1848 after which his two year authorization ended and the gate was operated by successors. The year the gate opened Barlow collected the toll for 145 wagons, 1559 horses, mules, oxen, and cattle, and about 1300 sheep. Although traffic increased each year thereafter, Sam Barlow's costs greatly exceeded the tolls he collected and his part in the venture was never profitable. The toll was the first on the Oregon Trail, but not the last. In 1853 four additional toll gates were established along the route Barlow created. The Barlow Road was rough and steep and there was little grass for the livestock, but it was still a cheaper and safer alternative than floating wagons and family down the Columbia River.

Captain Billy made a count of the wagons, horses, and animal teams while the train was on the trail and paid the toll for this group from the train's common fund prior to its arrival at the gate. He and the toll takers would have to count each cow as it passed the gate to get an accurate count of the cattle. Their toll would be paid from a separate kitty provided by those with a stake in the herd. Once everyone and everything had passed the gate, the train camped for the night at the first acceptable site it came to.

While making his daily check on the cowboy injured by the mule, Doc Brookings began to suspect something was wrong. It had been four days since the accident occurred and his patient did not seem to be getting any better at all. It was during the eye test that Brookings realized the cowboy was intentionally failing the tests, presumably to prolong the attention and other perks enjoyed by the sick and injured. Brookings accused the man of milking his injury and made him an offer. If he returned to work the day after next, his attempt to malinger would be their secret. Doc threw in the day of grace just to be sure the man was ready for duty. It was an offer the man had to accept. The next day would be Jacob Miller's last as a cowboy for now.

That same night the Walshes and the Marshalls had dinner together and, after cleaning up the pots and tin plates, sat around a common campfire discussing the future while Missy and Sarah entertained Angus. Angus was expending the last of his energy darting around the fire when he finally flopped down with his tail just a little too close to the flames. It was only a few seconds before the hair on his tail was ablaze. The girls saw it happen before Angus was even aware of his predicament and began screaming, "Angus is on fire! Angus is on fire!"

John Marshall reacted instantly, wrapping the little dog in his arms, pressing him against his chest, and smothering the flames. John's quick action spared Angus little more than a badly scorched tail and butt. With the smell of burnt hair in the air and wisps of smoke rising from John's shirt, everyone breathed a sigh of relief. "That could have been a lot worse," John remarked.

Neva thanked John several times before adding, "Your shirt is ruined. Add one to what we already owe you."

After conducting a thorough examination of Angus' posterior, Missy reported that he had suffered no serious burns, but stopped short of saying what she was thinking, that his rear end was not a very pretty sight. "I hope it grows back soon," she whispered to Sarah.

Unfazed by the experience, but aware that something significant had just happened, Angus looked sheepishly at Neva as if to say, "What did I do wrong?"

The next day the train traveled up the eastern slopes of the Cascades, forded the White River, and made camp for the night on the western side of the river. The river got its name from the color of the water that ran milky white in late summer and early fall when it carried glacial sediments from the melting Mount Hood snowpack. Those that counted on the river for water were asking Captain Billy and each other if the water was safe to drink. Doc Brookings declared the water safe for bathing and washing clothes, but advised against cooking with it or drinking too much of it. "It won't kill you, but I'm not sure it won't make you sick," was his conclusion. Ryan Walsh found the river very "fishy" looking, but decided to pass due to the unnatural color of the water. With only a week or so left on the trail, Captain Billy suggested to everyone that they leave any unneeded supplies behind at this point to minimize the effort required to pass through the Cascades. Some did and some did not. Parting with personal items and other nonessential things they had carried this far was asking a lot.

The next day the train continued to work its way up the mountain, following Barlow Creek upstream into a dense forest on the eastern side of Barlow Pass, the name given to the point at which the Barlow Road passed over the summit at an altitude of 4100 feet. Captain Billy stopped the train for the day just short of the summit at a location where the cattle and animal teams could feed on a broad expanse of lush grasses. The steady climb up the eastern slope wasn't difficult, but Billy knew the trail was extremely steep and rocky on the downhill side and that every trick learned earlier in the trip would be needed to negotiate the descent safely.

Early the next morning the descent began. Fallen trees were everywhere on the heavily forested trail, but the saw cut trunks lying along the side of the trail indicated that the train was the beneficiary of the trail clearing efforts of those traveling ahead of it. It was becoming increasimgly apparent that Billy's earlier statement that the Blue Mountains represented the train's last major obstacle was not entirely true and he wondered now how many of the emigrants still remembered those words. The spectacular view of snow-capped Mount Hood that emerged as the train moved slowly down the trail lessened somewhat the burden of the descent. Mount Hood is a potentially active volcano standing 11,250 feet above sea level at its peak. It last erupted in the 1790s although several minor tremors have been recorded since.

The train reached another popular stopover point known as Summit Meadow late in the afternoon and made camp there for the night. That evening Dewdrop was sitting with Missy and Sarah near the Marshall campfire getting her belly rubbed when Missy proclaimed, "I think Dewdrop's nipples are getting bigger!" Missy would have known as it was her who rubbed Dewdrop's stomach for at least a few minutes whenever Dewdrop came to visit.

Missy called her father over to take a look and, without hesitation, John said, "That dog's pregnant."

The faces of the two girls lit up immediately. To be sure, Missy asked her father to clarify his remark, "Do you mean we're going to have puppies?"

 Rolling his eyes, John answered, "What do you mean "we"?"

John called Ryan Walsh over to confirm his diagnosis. "I agree," Ryan said. "Look at that belly. She's the only one around here gaining weight." Ryan then turned to Angus who was sitting with Neva only a few yards away and asked, "Angus, do you know anything about this?"

"Oh stop," Neva calmly stated, "It had to be Rambles." The news spread quickly among those who knew Dewdrop. That it was a surprise to the cowboys was a surprise to everyone else. The boys treated Dewdrop a little differently from that day on.

The next morning the train reached a deserted encampment the emigrants called Government Camp. A year earlier a westbound U.S.

cavalry expedition was caught in a winter storm and forced to abandon its wagons at the site. The cavalry wagons were still there when Billy's train passed, but any useful items that may have been left behind by the troops were long gone.

Later that same day, the train came to the Laurel Hill Chute, easily the steepest downhill slope the train would see on the entire trip. The hill was nearly vertical in places. The animal teams were unhitched and guided down or around the chute separately. The wagons had to be lowered to the bottom with ropes and pulleys. The larger and heavier wagons were partially unloaded to reduce their weights to manageable amounts.

The operation was going well under Captain Billy's supervision until, with only a few wagons still at the top of the chute, one of the two ropes holding back a descending wagon snapped. The second rope alone could have handled the entire weight of the wagon if it had not pulled free of its anchor under the strain, allowing the wagon to tumble unrestrained down the hill. The wagon bounced around on the rocks and off to one side of the chute, landing directly on an unwary immigrant standing well below and, one would have thought, safely out of the way.

The poor woman never saw it coming and was killed the instant the wagon hit her. It all happened within a few seconds right before Billy's eyes. There was nothing Doc Brookings could do when he reached the woman but console her husband and son who were kneeling over her body weeping. It was heartbreaking, indeed, for the family to have come this far only to have their dreams crushed so near the end of the trip.

The Laurel Hill Chute

Moving the last few wagons down the chute under the circumstances was an uncomfortable task. Those that descended earlier in the day had moved to a nearby campsite and were already settled in for the night. Many used the extra time to call on the grieving family to offer their condolences. Captain Billy instructed the cowboys to dig a grave and construct a cross and announced that the funeral would be held the next morning. Billy's investigation of the incident was a short one. The rope that had failed was worn and frayed where it had broken from sliding back and forth against the rough bark of a tree used as part of the restraining system. The wear had gone unnoticed by those working at the top of the chute. It was yet another lesson learned too late.

Following the early morning funeral, the train broke camp and traveled along the south bank of the Sandy River. Although the trail was rough, it was at least reasonably level and there were no delays. The train forded the Sandy above its confluence with the Salmon River late in the day and made camp for the night on the river's north shore.

The next day the train passed the Rock Corral, a campsite at which arriving trains circled their wagons around a huge rock outcropping to prepare for the tricky trip along the Devil's Backbone. Captain Billy's scout reported that another train was already camped at the site and, since it was still early in the afternoon, he decided to push on and make camp closer to the last test of what was left of the emigrants' strength and stamina, a seven mile climb atop a narrow ridge where any misstep could prove disastrous. Billy figured it would take an entire day to negotiate the Devil's Backbone.

The campsite east of the Backbone was located in a dense forest. There was plenty of wood, but no water and no open space to circle the wagons or corral the cattle. The wagons were more or less scattered among the trees. Some just remained on the trail. Once everyone had found a place to stop, Captain Billy decided to ride around the encampment to figure out how best to keep the herd together. He was not far from the cattle when he noticed Rambles hopping wildly in circles and biting at his back. As soon as Billy pointed Bucket toward the dancing dog, Bucket began acting the same way and, looking down for a clue, Billy saw an army of yellow jackets streaming out of the ground. A second later they were on his legs.

Captain Billy and Bucket

Bucket took off without any coaxing from Billy with Rambles close on his heels. The two must have raced a hundred yards before Billy regained control of the situation and, confident the bees were no longer following, dismounted to assess the damage. He picked a dozen or more dead bees out of Rambles coat, saw that Bucket had numerous welts on each of his legs, and stopped counting the stings on his legs at the point where he could raise his pant legs no higher. A full count came a short time later when Billy dropped his drawers for Doc Brookings. "They stung me right through my pants!" Billy exclaimed.

Doc seemed to know quite a bit about the insects, informing Billy, "They're really wasps you know, not bees. They're very aggressive. They'll chase an intruder quite a distance and inflict a painful sting." Doc gave Billy a salve of some kind to apply to his stings and, if he could find them, to those on Rambles and Bucket as well. Doc added, "If it's any consolation to you, all but the queen will be dead in a month or two."

"It ain't," Billy replied.

Later that night Jesse noticed both Billy and Rambles scratching like crazy and asked, "What's the problem, fleas?"

"No. Bees," was Billy's terse reply. Jesse didn't question Billy further.

Travel along the Devil's Backbone was every bit as challenging as Captain Billy remembered it. In places the falloff on both sides of the trail was only a foot or two away from the wheels of the wagons. The emigrants had to walk ahead of their teams rather than beside them and tried to look straight ahead most of the time. The Backbone was not a place for anyone who suffered from a fear of heights. With the exception of a few that were unable to walk long distances, no one dared to ride on or in the wagons. The train moved slowly and deliberately along the ridge and made it over the most hazardous part of the Backbone without incident.

It was only after the trail became wider and the slope on each side less severe that a weary, older man stumbled over the edge, dragging his wife along with him as she tried to hold him back. The two were fortunate, coming to rest after tumbling only twenty yards from the trail. After being helped back to their wagon by those nearby, Doc Brookings was summoned to their location to patch up their cuts and bruises. Although both could walk, Doc suspected that the woman, who was in great pain, may have broken her collarbone and perhaps a few ribs as well. He would conduct a more thorough examination once the train had stopped for the day in order to keep the delay relatively short as it wasn't possible for one wagon to pass another on this narrow stretch of trail.

The train came to a good site less than an hour after clearing the Devil's Backbone and made camp there for the night. Shortly after the train stopped, Doc Brookings called on the woman injured in the fall and, after probing and pressing all of the painful areas, concluded that she may have nicked her collarbone, but that it was not broken. Two or three of her ribs, however, appeared to be cracked. "There's not much I can do for you. The ribs will mend on their own," Doc told her. Knowing that she would have trouble breathing and sleeping for a while, he gave her one small dose of morphine for the pain. "Take this after dinner. It will help you sleep," Doc instructed her, "and let me know if you need any more tomorrow night." Because the drug was highly addictive, Doc didn't tell her what it was and would encourage her to take as little as possible. The addictive power of the drug became widely recognized twenty years later when it was estimated that as many as 400,000 American Civil War veterans suffered from "soldier's disease", a euphemism for morphine addiction.

Waiting for the call to dinner, Missy and Sarah were over at the Walsh wagon checking on Angus' condition when Dewdrop made her evening appearance. Both dogs appeared to be exhausted and wanted only to lay stretched out on their sides for petting. Caressing Dewdrop's belly, Missy thought she felt something move, but wasn't quite sure of it. She leaned over, pressed her hand firmly against Dewdrop's abdomen, and waited for something to happen. "Yes. Something's moving in there!" she whispered to Sarah. Sarah took her turn and confirmed Missy's observation. That was all Missy needed to suggest to Sarah, "Let's make a list of names for the puppies."

From the Devil's Backbone, the Barlow Road ran downhill to the Sandy River where the train crossed it for a second time. One of two crossing points could be used to ford the river. The first was a gravel bar that was exposed when the water level was low. The second was a riverbed which was generally quite shallow in the summer months. Captain Billy chose the gravel bar and the crossing was a quick and easy one. After crossing the Sandy, the train headed back uphill, arriving at their last stopover before reaching Oregon City with a few hours of daylight still remaining. It was Philip Foster's Farm in Eagle Creek. One of Oregon's earliest settlers, Foster was instrumental in many of the improvements to the Barlow Road that were made during the period 1848 to 1865. The farm remains in operation today as a historic site and tourist attraction. Here the emigrants could rest, buy food, and, for the lucky ones who had a little money and time to spare, eat some of Mrs. Foster's home cooking.

Another train was already camped at the farm when Captain Billy's group arrived, but there was plenty of room for additional arrivals to camp in comfort. The mood of the emigrants was upbeat with only one tick left on the countdown of days on the trail. Billy and Rambles had dinner with Jesse, Dewdrop, and the cowboys. They ate generous portions of beef that Billy had just bought at the Foster Farm store. Doc Brookings, the Marshalls, and the Walshes ate together at the Marshall wagon, sharing a fine supper that included a number of the special treats that John Marshall had purchased along the way. There was no reason to save them any longer.

After dinner Doc and Neva walked hand in hand around the farm until well after dark, reviewing the five month long journey they were about to complete. As their walk was about to end, Doc became uncharacteristically nervous and, with his trembling hand holding hers, popped the question, "Neva, will you marry me?" It was a question Neva hoped might someday come and, although she had rehearsed her reply more than once in her mind, hesitated just long enough to create a little suspense before answering, "Yes, James, of course I will." Doc sealed the deal with a kiss. The two then made the decision to wait until the train finally reached Oregon City to announce their engagement to the others. Neva slept more soundly that night than Doc did.

It was the end of September when the train entered Abernethy Green, a large meadow located behind Governor George Abernathy's house and the official end of the Oregon Trail. It would be the last campground the emigrants would occupy as a group. Soon after the campfires were lit, everyone was celebrating the end of the journey in groups small and large with friends made along the way. No one was asking if the rules of the train were still in effect and more than a few were drinking hard and fast.

The End of the Trail – Arrival in Oregon City

Captain Billy, Doc Brookings, the Marshalls and the Walshes sat together sharing their most memorable experiences on the trail. All of the dogs were there as well – Angus with his hairless hiney, Rambles scratching his stings, and Dewdrop bulging with a litter of pups. The gatherings nearby grew louder and more boisterous until it became difficult to talk over the surrounding din. "They've earned it," Billy said, "I just hope things don't get too rowdy."

Unable to keep her secret to herself any longer, Neva Walsh waited for a pause in the conversation, rose to her feet, and practically shouted over the nearby noise, "I have an announcement. James and I are getting married!"

"Who's James?" John Marshall joked.

Ryan Walsh was not surprised, but wondered now how Neva's marriage would affect his future. John quickly went to his wagon, rummaged around for a few seconds, and returned to the circle with a bottle of French champagne. "This calls for a toast," John said as he worked to uncork the bottle.

Amazed that John possessed such a rarity, Billy couldn't refrain from asking, "John, what else do you have hidden in that wagon?" Doc sat smiling throughout John's eloquent toast, his flushed face masked by the glow of the campfire.

Later that evening Billy and Doc raised their cups one last time to remember those who had died on the trail. "I think it was eleven, not counting the rustler and the dog," Billy said.

"Yes, that's right, but from what I've read, that's not bad," Doc replied. It was, in fact, not bad at all.

The next morning the emigrants rose slowly and spent time saying their goodbyes and exchanging plans to meet with friends at some point in the future. Most, however, would go their own way, some to build homes in Oregon City, some to establish farms in the valley, and some continuing northwest to settle near the mouth of the Willamette River. Billy and the cowboys had three remaining responsibilities to take care of that morning. The first was to return to each emigrant his share of the small amount of money that remained in the train's common fund. The second was to allocate the cattle among those with an ownership interest in the herd. The third was to decide the fates of Dewdrop and Rambles.

Missy Marshall's fondness for Dewdrop was no secret and Missy was not about to let her drift off as a stray. With Sarah as her audience, she had rehearsed her pitch to keep Dewdrop several times and was ready to make her formal plea as soon as her father was awake. John Marshall knew it was coming and had already decided to say yes, but feigned being groggy after rising to create a little drama. After mulling Missy's emotional appeal over for a minute or two, John finally said, "If it makes you happy Missy, Dewdrop is yours. Go find her and bring her back for breakfast."

Relieved and delighted, Missy and Sarah quickly finished dressing and ran off in the direction of the cattle. There they found Jesse and the cowboys drinking coffee and Dewdrop waiting for her morning bacon. Jesse had given a lot of thought to taking Dewdrop along with him, but her pregnancy made the notion much too complicated. He was happy to see her going to a farm with Missy and Sarah to have her puppies. Jesse and each of the cowboys gave Dewdrop a big hug to thank her for her company and her service. There were even a few kisses on the head and a wet eye or two. As the girls led Dewdrop away, Jesse stroked what had been her tail and shouted after them, "Don't be surprised if I come to visit her someday."

After distributing what was left of the train's funds, Captain Billy checked the two supply wagons to see what they still held. Almost all of the food and other consumables were gone. One wagon contained mostly tools, ropes, and spare parts. The second contained little but Doc Brookings' medical supplies. Billy and Doc would each take a wagon and the animal team that pulled it as partial compensation for their services. As the two discussed the arrangement, Doc noticed the other unresolved issue sitting patiently nearby – Rambles. "What about the dog, Billy?" Doc asked.

Billy looked the dog in the eye and with little hesitation said, "Come here, Rambles." Rambles got to his feet and slowly walked in Billy's direction. When he got within reach, Billy pulled Rambles to his chest and gave him a big hug, the first Rambles had ever received from him. "Let's stick it out together old boy," Billy said, "I don't want to live alone and I'm sure you'll be less trouble than a wife." By noon the campsite was deserted. Billy, Bucket, and Rambles were the last to leave.

CHAPTER 13 - NEW BEGINNINGS

Located 15 miles south of the present day city of Portland, Oregon City was founded in 1842 by Dr. John McLoughlin, the same fellow who ran the Hudson's Bay Company at Fort Vancouver. He chose the site because it was located just below the Willamette River falls. The falls prevented any river travel south of the city and provided power for McLoughlin's commercial sawmill. In 1844 Oregon City became the seat of the new American Provisional Government. By 1850 Oregon's emigrant population had grown to more than 13,000 while the number of native Indians living just in the Willamette Valley shrank from 14,000 to only about a thousand during the period 1800 to 1850. A great many died in a malaria epidemic in the 1830s. The Indians were now a minority in the area around Oregon City.

Before parting company at Abernathy Green, Captain Billy and Jesse arranged to meet at one of the local saloons to discuss their tentative plan to ride back to Missouri together. Each man had indicated to the other that he would be returning to Independence to work on another wagon train the following spring. At their meeting, however, Billy informed Jesse that the physical stress and burden of responsibility of leading yet another train west was not really what he wanted. He planned instead to accept a job as the manager of a large cattle ranch located in the valley. "The pay's good, the owner's nice, and the job includes room and board," Billy said, staring blankly into his glass of beer.

"That's all fine, but you don't seem very excited about it," Jesse replied.

Billy confessed that he was willing to forego excitement for contentment and added, "Besides, I don't think either Bucket or Rambles are up to another round trip on the trail."

"Ha! I got it now. You've gone soft!" Jesse joked. Billy told Jesse that there was a job on the ranch for him if he was interested, but Jesse was intent on returning to Independence. He hoped to parlay what he had learned from Billy on this last trip into a position as captain of the next train for which he worked. Billy wished him luck and offered to write Jesse a letter of recommendation. Then the two emptied their glasses together, shook hands, and went their separate ways.

Within a week of arriving in the valley, John Marshall filed the paperwork needed to legally adopt Sarah. Missy and Sarah had become inseparable friends and it was almost inevitable that Sarah would become her sister as well. Realizing that the Marshalls represented the best possible future for her, Sarah did her best to impress John and Emma

196

during their time together on the trail and, as it turned out, had played her cards just right. As John put it, "She's a sweet kid, an extra pair of hands, and will keep Missy busy while we're working." Emma agreed, noting that it was much too late for her to produce a sibling that would interest Missy as much as Sarah did. Missy couldn't wait to have Sarah practice writing her new name, Sarah Marshall.

regon City on the Willamette River Circa 1850

(1850 painting by John Mix Stanley)

The Marshalls and the Walshes spent the first few days in the valley studying maps and visiting available plots of desirable farmland. The newly adopted Donation Land Claim Act of 1850 allowed new arrivals to claim 320 acres of farmland as a single person or 640 acres if they were married on the condition that the land was "improved" by the claimant. One needed only to build a permanent structure and cultivate and plant 20 acres to satisfy the requirement. There was still plenty of land available in 1850, but due to the steady stream of emigrants and the Land Claim Act most of the good agricultural land in the valley was gone less than a decade later.

Ryan Walsh claimed land about three miles from town, but only a few hundred yards from the Willamette River and the bounty it held for a fisherman. He also sold three of the four oxen that pulled his wagon from Independence and, with the proceeds, bought a horse, a bridle, and a saddle. The horse was an absolute necessity for getting around the valley and, although he had little experience on horseback, Ryan was riding it confidently within a week.

With some financial help from Doc Brookings, Ryan planned to build a modest, but comfortable two room log cabin with a large fireplace, a sleeping loft, and front and back door porches. He would do most of the work himself, working practically around the clock to get himself under roof before the cold weather arrived. A small, winter stable for his horse and the remaining oxen would be added to the south wall once the cabin was done. In the meantime, he and Neva would camp out on the site until Neva's wedding in early November after which she would join her new husband in Oregon City and Ryan would be left to live alone. Although Neva's help would last only a month, Ryan hoped it would move the construction of the cabin along quickly. During their last month together the two had to decide with whom Angus would live. If left up to him they thought, would he choose a comfortable, domesticated life in the city with

Doc and Neva or an outdoor life on the farm with only Ryan and the local varmints for company?

Once John Marshall had chosen a location for his farm, he moved his family into two small rooms in an Oregon City guest house where he worked non-stop on plans for his new house and the layout of the barns, sheds, fence lines, and so on that a working farm of the size he envisioned would need. He would be a hands on laborer as well as the general contractor, but hired a skilled builder with several helpers to get the house partially done and habitable as soon as possible. He hoped to have the house completely finished and furnished in time for Christmas.

The first order of business for Doc Brookings was to obtain a bank loan and, given the potential for a doctor in a rapidly expanding city, his creditworthiness was unquestioned by the local banker. Doc found a building for sale on the main street of Oregon City, a perfect location in which to establish his medical practice. The building had ample living quarters on the second floor for his family to be and two small rooms in addition to the examination and waiting rooms on the first floor that could be outfitted as hospital or recovery rooms. His loan ended up being larger than he actually needed, but the terms were favorable and the additional funds could be used to help Ryan get started. His first employee, of course, would be Neva who would join him following their wedding as both his wife and his assistant. Doc was confident that the valley's growing population and the arrival of a steady stream of sick and injured emigrants would result in a thriving and highly profitable practice.

About two weeks into their stay at the guest house, Missy Marshall called her father to the room in which she and Sarah and Dewdrop slept and announced, "Father, I think it's time!" Unaccustomed to such cramped quarters, Dewdrop had been exhibiting signs of anxiety for days, but was acting unusually strange on this day and Missy correctly concluded that she was now ready to have her pups. John took a seat across the room, ready to assist her if she needed any help.

Although this was apparently her first litter, Dewdrop handled most of the motherly details on her own. The puppies came about twenty minutes apart, five of them in all, under the watchful eyes of Missy and Sarah. Emma Marshall joined the group as the first pup was being born and, together with John, recognized that sharing the excitement and joy of the girls as each pup arrived was a very special event. There were four females and one male born that evening.

Four days had passed before Missy and Sarah felt they knew the pups well enough to name them. They had developed a lengthy list of names in advance and needed only to match the pups to the appropriate male and female names on their list. The only male and the pup that looked most like his father was given the name Scrambles. The pup that looked most like her mother was named Raindrop. They named the pup with the bluest eyes and a coat that was mostly white Snowflake. The smallest of the five pups was given the name Teardrop. The girls named the fourth female Gumdrop because they thought she was the sweetest pup of them all.

The pups were only a week old when it became obvious that Teardrop, unlike the others, was growing weaker each day. The special attention she received from Dewdrop and the girls was not enough to save her and she died at the age of ten days. Although he knew it was a hopeless gesture, John Marshall even sought the help of Doc Brookings to make Missy and Sarah feel that every effort to save the poor pup had been made. The girls dug a grave not far from the guest house and buried Teardrop themselves the day she died with John and Emma looking on.

On the first Sunday afternoon in November, Doc and Neva were married. The ceremony was held in the local church and was attended by the Marshalls, Captain Billy, Ryan, and, at the insistence of the newlyweds, Dewdrop, Rambles, and Angus. It was the first reunion of the three dogs since they had left Abernathy Green. Doc and Neva were dressed resplendently, he in a brand new suit and she in a beautiful white gown, a wedding gift from the Marshalls.

As the couple exchanged vows, Emma Marshall, Neva's maid of honor, stood to her left, and Doc's best man, Billy, stood to his right. Missy and Sarah were, of course, the flower girls. They spent the entire morning combing nearby fields for whatever late season blooms they could find and surprised everyone with the large and colorful arrangements they managed to put together. Once the groom had kissed the bride and the short burst of clapping and barking ended, everyone walked the short distance to the couple's new home for the reception. The group's parade down Main Street in wedding garb, led by the preacher, drew a continuous chorus of cheers from onlookers out for a Sunday stroll.

Mr. and Mrs. James Brookings

Once the food and drinks were laid out, the preacher presented Doc and Neva with the "Book of Advice", a traditional gift from the presiding clergyman that presumably addressed all of a newly married couple's questions and problems. Doc graciously accepted the book and passed it along to Neva, winking as he did so and whispering in her ear, "Why don't you read it first and tell me what I'm doing wrong."

As his gift, Billy gave Neva a matching bracelet and necklace made of intricately carved walrus ivory and black slate. They were stunning works of art made by a local Indian craftsman. Turning to the groom, Billy stated apologetically, "Sorry, Doc. I couldn't find anything I thought would look good on you."

The celebration lasted well into the evening before the guests respectfully left the newlyweds to do what newlyweds do on their first night together. As Ryan headed for the door, Angus wasn't sure which way to turn, and looked to each of his owners for direction. Neva and Ryan decided to let Angus make the choice, knowing that if his decision wasn't a good one, it could later easily be reversed. Angus waited until Ryan was almost out of the door before trotting after him. Neva was not disappointed. After all, she had already had a pretty good day and felt more than a little responsible for leaving Ryan on his own. Ryan held Angus tightly in his lap on the chilly ride home, thankful for the companionship his little fishing buddy would provide.

Billy was now settled into his new job and becoming more satisfied with his decision to stay in the valley with each passing day. He hired Jacob Miller and two of the more responsible cowboys to round out the ranch's work force. Jacob's father was a tradesman and so Jacob was not needed to work on a family farm and chose to go his own way, at least for a while, rather than become his father's apprentice. These hires helped knit the entire group of ranch hands together.

Rambles split his time between Billy and Jacob, spending most of the working day with Jacob and most off duty hours with Billy, an arrangement that seemed to suit all three just fine. The ranch was close enough to Oregon City for Jacob to visit his family every Sunday with church and a big dinner highlighting his weekly visit. Jacob's mother worried only that the cowboy lifestyle rather than church teachings would end up ruling his behavior.

Construction on the Marshall house was far enough along by late November for the family to move from the guest house and take up residence there. Although there was still a lot of work to be done, John and Emma decided to host a Thanksgiving dinner and invited the Brookings, Billy, and Ryan Walsh to the affair. Although it was not yet an official holiday in Oregon, by 1850 almost every state and territory celebrated Thanksgiving. It did not become a national holiday until Abraham Lincoln declared it one in 1863, in part to heal the scars of the Civil War. Even then, it was not made a permanent holiday. The President had to proclaim it as one every year. Over time, the last Thursday in November became its customary date.

Emma would have served the dishes traditionally associated with Thanksgiving in Ohio if it were not for the fact that things like apples and turkeys and other basic ingredients were just not available in Oregon. There was, however, enough warm eggnog and hot spiced rum that no one thought much about the menu. Fresh eggs were rare, but somehow a few hearty birds made it to Oregon and John found the only chicken farm in the valley. The birds that left Independence on Billy's train lasted only a few weeks before they stopping laying and became dinner.

The Thanksgiving gathering was another opportunity for Rambles, Dewdrop, and Angus to reunite, but this reunion was different. Dewdrop's four puppies were now six weeks old and, once given the run of the house, Missy and Sarah proudly introduced each by name to those seeing them for the first time. They were delightful entertainment for the guests and relentless in their attempts to coax Rambles and Angus into playing with them. Rambles' nose told him there was something special about these pups, but other than tolerating their playful advances, he seemed altogether indifferent to them. Dewdrop sat off to the side watching as the pups met their father for the first time. "See," Missy said, "Don't Rambles and Scrambles look alike."

"It doesn't look like Rambles is ready to confess to anything," Billy chuckled.

A few weeks later John Marshall informed Missy and Sarah that it was time to find new homes for the puppies. They were no longer nursing and John knew that the longer they were around the more difficult it would be to part with them. Missy had already convinced her father to let her keep one of the pups, but was angling now for a second so that she and Sarah could each have one. The debate ended when Emma cast her vote to keep two. John was thinking about the amount of food three large dogs would require, but reluctantly agreed to honor the three to one vote.

Gumdrop, Raindrop, and Snowflake

Scrambles

Gumdrop and Snowflake were the keepers. Missy was in charge of interviewing and approving the prospective owners of the others. The process was quite thorough, much more so than that leading to Sarah's adoption, but there was enough interest among the local farm families that good homes were soon found for Scrambles and Raindrop. Two of Missy's requirements were that the new owners keep the names she had given them and that she and Sarah had a perpetual right of visitation.

By the middle of December, Ryan Walsh's cabin was finished. It was much nicer than Neva thought it would be and worthy of a housewarming party that she would plan and service. It was attended only by the Marshalls and the Brookings with Neva and Emma bringing the food and doing the cooking. John Marshall presented Ryan with a housewarming gift, a fishing rod. This was not just any fishing rod, but one made from Calcutta cane in Bavaria, and it was complimented by a bait casting reel, one of the first gear multiplying reels available at the time. The combination represented the very latest in fishing technology. Ryan was speechless. "Let's see a dog outfish you now," John remarked.

The Marshall's house was completed just in time for Christmas as planned. It was one the largest farm houses in the valley. John and Emma spent that Christmas Eve sitting contentedly in front of the fireplace watching the girls and the dogs, thankful that most of the hard work associated with the move west was behind them. John spent the winter months preparing the farm for commercial operation. By spring the barns and the other outbuildings were in place, a water well had been dug, several acres of pasture had been fenced, and the land to be planted had been tilled.

As the planting seasons arrived, he planted wheat, corn, and potatoes, crops with which he was familiar, as well as oats and barely. These were his cash crops. He purchased half a dozen dairy cows, a flock of sheep, and, of course, some pigs and sold the milk, lamb, and pork the family did not consume to the local markets. John also planted plum and apple orchards from the first seedlings to reach northern Oregon. In addition to their usual chores, Missy and Sarah were responsible for nurturing the young trees and were the first in the valley to harvest these fruits.

By midsummer, Snowflake and Gumdrop were nearly as large as their mother and kept busy harassing the livestock, patrolling the farm with Dewdrop, and playing with the girls. John Marshall's vision of life in Oregon had been realized.

It was the trappers and missionaries who led the way west. They were followed by those with the courage and determination to pull up roots, leave their families, and risk everything for the chance to live a better life in the west. The early emigrants, in turn, proved to the hundreds of thousands to follow that the risk was worth taking. In the process, the country was unified and Manifest Destiny, the notion that the expansion was "divinely ordained", was realized. With the introduction of bridges, ferries, and steamboats, and the development of trading and military posts along the way, the journey became safer and less demanding as the years went by. Completion of the first transcontinental railroad in 1869 marked the beginning of the end of travel along the overland migration routes. The wagon ruts, however, still remain as reminders of the era.

THE END

(Appendices A through D follow)

APPENDIX A – THE COST OF THE TRIP WEST (A FAMILY OF FOUR)

Item	Cost in 1850	Cost in 2017 Dollars
Wagon and animal team:		
Six Mules @ $100 each.	$600	$18,060
Six Oxen @ $50 per pair.	$150	$4,515
Prairie Schooner type wagon.	$85	$2,558
Cover for wagon.	$100	$3,010
Food for a family of four:		
500 lb. bacon @ $0.10 per lb.	$50	$1,505
12 sacks of flour @ $3.00 per sack.	$36	$1,084
200 lb. sugar @ $0.10 per lb.	$20	$602
100 lb. lard @ $0.07 per lb.	$7	$211
100 lb. coffee @ $0.25 per lb.	$25	$752
5 bushels dried fruit @ $2.00 per bushel.	$10	$301
2 bushels beans @ $1.50 per bushel	$3	$90
100 lb. rice @ $0.05 per lb.	$5	$151
50 lb. salt and pepper.	$2	$60
Cornmeal, vinegar, molasses, yeast, dried beef.	$20	$602
Fees, equipment, and other supplies:		
Cooking utensils, stove, water cask, churn.	$30	$903
Tolls, ferry fees, common expenses.	$50 (No cattle)	$1,505
Cost of supplies purchased along the way.	$50	$1,505
Wagon train fee.	$75	$2,257
Clothing, tent, and bedding.	$40	$1,204
Tools, equipment, rope, spare parts.	$25	$752
Hunting rifle and ammunition	$100	$3,010
Medical supplies; miscellaneous	$15	$451
Total (for a wagon pulled by six mules)	**$1,348**	**$40,5758**
Total (for a wagon pulled by six oxen)	**$898**	**$27,030**

Note: $1.00 in 1850 was equivalent to $30.10 in 2017.

APPENDIX B – WHERE DID ALL THE ANIMALS GO?

Species	Population Before the West Was Settled (Before 1800)	What Happened to Them?	Approximate Population at the low point	Approximate Population Today
American Bison	60,000,000	Hunted for food and hides; indiscriminate slaughter for sport only.	1,000 (1889). The population was 25,000,000 in 1840 and 5,500,000 in 1870.	About 500,000 - 30,000 purebred & wild; 5,000 fenced; 465,000 cross-bred with cattle.
Grey Wolf	250,000 to 500,000 Once found in every continental US state and Alaska.	Trapped and shot in systematic extermination campaigns; loss of 90% of habitat to human encroachment.	Oregon - None (1950). Continental US – 300 (1960). Found only in the deep woods of upper MI & MN.	Oregon -120. Alaska – 10,000. Continental US – 5,700. First to repopulate OR migrated from ID.
North American Beaver	400,000,000	Unregulated trapping for fur & castor glands (used in medicines and perfumes).	100,000	Approx. 15,000,000
Elk	10,000,000	Unregulated hunting; loss of habitat due to westward expansion; grazing competition w/ domestic livestock.	<100,000 (1890)	Approx. 1,000,000
Salmon in Idaho	Spawning in Idaho: Sockeye – 150,000. Chinook – 120,000.	Dam construction (15 dams on the Snake River); agricultural runoff; rising water temperatures.	Hell's Canyon Dam on Idaho-Oregon border blocks passage to the Snake River in ID entirely. No native fish.	Recovery programs, transport projects, & hatchery fish have produced a local population of Sockeye.
Prairie Dog	300,000,000 to 1,000,000,000	Poisoned and shot by farmers (interfere with cattle ranching); many died of sylvatic plague; loss of 95% of habitat to human encroachment.		10,000,000 to 20,000,000

Note: Population statistics are for the continental United States unless otherwise noted.

APPENDIX C - 38 WAYS TO DIE ON THE TRAIL

Category	Cause of Death	Comments
Weather	Struck by lightning. Pummeled by hail. Exposure to heat. Exposure to cold. Drowned in a flash flood. Stranded in heavy snow.	
Diseases	Cholera. Smallpox. Influenza. Measles. Mumps. Tuberculosis. Dysentery. Premature burial.	Bad water, poor sanitary conditions, lack of medical treatment, living in groups, and no quarantine of the sick. These factors in combination made any illness potentially fatal.
River Crossings	Drowned in an overturned wagon. Swept away trying to swim across.	Few ferries and no bridges were in operation in 1850.
Wagon Accidents	Run over by a wagon. Wagon falling over a cliff. Being thrown around inside a wagon.	
Conflicts with Indians	Shot by an arrow. Shot with a rifle. Beaten to death.	During the years 1840 to 1860: 362 emigrants killed by Indians. 460 Indians killed by emigrants.
Gunshot Accidents	Shot by an inexperienced hunter. Shot by nervous guards on night watch. Accidental discharge in bumpy wagon. Shot by stray bullet during a celebration.	
Animal Incidents	Trampled in a cattle stampede. Trampled in a buffalo stampede. Rattlesnake bite.	
Thieves and Rustlers	Shot by a rustler. Shot by a thief.	
Lack of Sustenance	Starvation. Food poisoning. Lack of water (dehydration).	
Mental Illness	Suicide. Killed by an insane person.	
Miscellaneous	Died during childbirth. Guide leads party the wrong way.	

Note: One of every ten emigrants who started the trip died on the trail.

APPENDIX D - SO MANY RIVERS TO CROSS

Located in the Present Day State of	Major River Crossings	Minor Creek and River Crossings
Missouri	Missouri River (For those traveling to Independence, Missouri by boat)	
Kansas	Blue River Wakarusa River Kansas River Vermillion River Big Blue River	
Nebraska	Little Blue River South Platte River	
Wyoming	Laramie River North Platte River Sweetwater River (nine crossings) Big Sandy River Green River	Horse Creek Cottonwood Creek La Bonte Creek Bad Tick Creek La Prele Creek Deer Creek Box Elder Creek Black's Fork Ham's Fork Fontenelle Creek
Idaho	Thomas Fork Bear River Raft River Snake River (at the Three Island Crossing) Boise River	Clover Creek Goose Creek Deep Creek Salmon Creek
Oregon	Snake River (at Old Fort Boise) Malheur River Burnt River (many crossings) Powder River Umatilla River John Day River Deschutes River Columbia River (For those traveling from The Dalles by boat) White River Sandy River (Lower Crossing) Sandy River (Upper Crossing) Clackamas River	Manning Creek Durkee Creek Lawrence Creek Wolf Creek Willow River Five Mile Creek Eight Mile Creek Fifteen Mile Creek

Note: Listing does not include many smaller creeks and river tributaries.

Made in United States
Orlando, FL
15 November 2021

10436609R00132